THE NAVY OF ... SQU...

BOOK 1

FIRE ANT

Colonel Jonathan P. Brazee
USMC (Ret)

Copyright © 2018 Jonathan Brazee

A Semper Fi Press Book

Copyright © 2018 Jonathan Brazee

ISBN-13: 978-1-945743-22-1
ISBN-10: 1-945743-22-0   (Semper Fi Press)

Printed in the United States of America

All rights reserved. No part of this book may be used or reproduced by any means, graphic, electronic, or mechanical, including photocopying, recording, taping or by any information storage retrieval system without the written permission of the publisher except in the case of brief quotations embodied in critical articles and reviews.

This is a work of fiction. All of the characters, names, incidents, organizations, and dialogue in this novel are either the products of the author's imagination or are used fictitiously.

Acknowledgements:
I want to thank all those who took the time to offer advice as I wrote this book. A special thanks goes my editor, Abbyedits, real Navy air warriors, CAPT Andrés "Drew" Brugal, USN, (Ret) and CAPT Timothy "Spike" Prendergast, USN (Ret.) for keeping helping me with "air-speak" and culture, and to my beta readers James Caplan and Kelly O'Donnell for their valuable input.

Cover by Jude Beers

DEDICATION

Airman 1st Class Elizabeth Jacobson, United States Air Force
Born 26 March 1984
KIA 28 Sept 2005. Basra, Iraq

and

First Lieutenant Albert H Westendorf, US Army Air Corps
Flew 55 missions as a B-25 Bombardier/ Navigator
Awarded the Distinguished Flying Cross
1921-2000

PART 1

Chapter 1

No bonus on this run, Beth told herself as she read the analysis.

Pilot Two Floribeth Salinas O'Shea Dalisay, Hamdani Exploration Corps, ran through her Hummingbird's diagnostics one more time, hoping that she'd missed something, but no. Another dry well.

Beth had been on a long run of dry wells since her last hit: sixteen missions, sixteen times without a bonus. With her expenses, all conveniently taken out of her pay by Hamdani Brothers, that left scant little to send home to her family. She *needed* a bonus.

There was no use wasting time hanging in the barren system. The data she'd collected had been uploaded to corps headquarters, so her work here was done.

She shifted her body in her harness. In zero-G, she didn't have bedsores per se, but she did have contact spots, irritation from where her harness and even her flight suit rubbed her. Her piss tube, which was hypo-allergenic and guaranteed not to irritate, felt like sandpaper. Her finger hovered over her console for a moment as she considered returning to the station. She'd been out for over 62 Standard days—1,494 hours, in fact—and that was a long time to be stuck in her Hummingbird, relying on drugs, nanos, and the devil the Hummingbird pilots called the "stretcher" to keep her muscles from atrophying. Her body cried to get out of her suit, to feel gravity, to walk, to stand naked in a shower as water jets scrubbed off the stink and itch of deep space. She needed the taste of a cold Coke to wash out the days of the food paste the pilots called "slime."

Can't make anything going back, she told herself. *Maybe the next one's it.*

With a heavy heart, she pressed the "Next Mission" button, waiting for HQ's response. Anagolay would be running her calculations, determining what system among the vast reaches of the galaxy, would offer the best probability of providing the raw materials that HB needed to fuel its factories. Even better than that, which system provided the best chance at an Alpha world, a planet that could host human life. This was the proverbial golden ring for the pilots of the Exploration Corps. Finding one would set up Beth for life. She could return to New Cebu and open up her own store. With her family's future secure, she could think about finding a husband and starting her own family, raising kids who would never have to leave New Cebu in order to make a living.

Light years away, Ana's circuits did their thing, and the AI sent out a response: SG-4021. The designation meant nothing to her. It was simply one more star system among the 100 billion in the galaxy. All the low-hanging fruit had long been plucked, systems where scans had indicated planets that could support life with minor or no terraforming required. Systems with easily harvested heavy metals had already been explored. Now, 400-plus years since the Grand Expansion, corporations, from the big zaibatsus such as Hamdani Brothers to small indies searched the black for other jewels to be exploited. Only a tiny fraction of the galaxy's systems had been explored, so no one knew what treasures were out there, waiting to be found.

By accepting the orders, Beth had just locked herself in the *Lily* for another 12 days at a minimum. The thought almost overwhelmed her, and she could swear her piss tube shifted, rubbing her raw.

She could have refused. The OPW Union, which was relatively powerless in most ways, had still managed to get some regulations enacted for deep-space pilots. Commercial pilots, those working for corporations, could only be required to conduct two missions before returning to their bases. Two missions, however, would barely pay for expenses for most of them. Beth wasn't a pilot for charity—her family needed the support. So, this would be Beth's fifth mission on this run.

The trip to SG-4021 would take place in two steps. First, she had to accelerate to a minimum of .54 of the speed of light before entering the gate. The transport back to Nexus Prime would take no sidereal time at all, and only a few moments to reach the next gate to take her to her destination. Then it would be the long deceleration process into the system proper where her scanners could analyze it.

The math was too complicated for a human brain to grasp, and Beth didn't even try. She trusted Ana's vast computing power and her little Hummingbird's ability to make the transit. Fly-by-night indies often got lost between systems, never to be heard from again, but not HB pilots. All of the pilots resented the zaibatsu's roughshod manner, but it was still one of the most competent. The HB Explorer Corps hadn't lost a Hummingbird in over nine years, which was one of the reasons Beth had accepted the contract with them. She had to endure the long, lonely trips in deep space, but she was not particularly brave. As a child and teen, she'd never been bit by the wanderlust bug. She was supporting her extended family, like most Off-Planet Workers, and that required her to survive the work.

New Cebu was a relatively poor world, with the wealth highly concentrated among the planet's Golden Tribe. The masses were dirt poor, but they were the planet's most valuable resource. They became the beasts of burden for all the jobs that the GT's wouldn't sully their precious skin with.

Beth stretched her legs as the *Lily*'s navigation system inputted the instructions. They didn't stretch far. Beth stood 4'6" in her bare feet (137 cm in Universal Standard) and weighed 72 pounds soaking wet (32.6 kgs). She'd always been the smallest girl in her class, but her size had plucked her out of housekeeping at the Montclair Resort on Bally's World to become a pilot in the HB Explorer Corps. She'd received bonuses on three of her first seven missions, earning more than she could have made throughout her 15-year housekeeping contract.

The money might be her primary motivation, but over time, Beth realized she liked being a pilot. Despite the long hours in her cramped cockpit, despite the lack of real food, of tubes to take care of her bodily waste, despite the loneliness, she felt at home in space. She liked flying her Hummingbird, of being the first human to enter new solar systems. She might long to get out of her little ship at the moment, and she was frustrated by her string of dry wells, but she was glad she wasn't cleaning toilets for rich folks anymore. Beth might still be an OPW, but she'd lucked into one of the best jobs someone from her background could have.

Her console command light turned green. She could still refuse the mission without penalty. Every pilot thought that canceling a mission after accepting it would have dire consequences. The pilots might have named Ana after the old Filipino goddess of lost travelers, but the AI belonged to HB, and she was programmed to improve the bottom line. It would not be beyond HB to punish those who canceled missions with systems that had a lower probability of earning the pilot a bonus.

She didn't hesitate. She pushed the command, then flipped down her entertainment screen. Bobo had sent her the link to a two-hundred-year-old feline opera series, and she'd been saving it so she could binge watch it.

She had the time for that now.

****

Beth ran through the checklist. If something were off, lights would be flashing red, but company policy was company policy, and HB *loved* checklists. She quickly scanned as she watched the timer count down until the *Lily* would enter the gate she'd left three days before. This might be the last time it was ever used. There hadn't been enough in the FR-30072 system to warrant another mission, but the law was the law, and not even the most powerful corporations would fight this. Once set, a gate remained in place, its coordinates logged. Anyone could use it, and unless HB registered a claim, anyone could make do with the system as they would.

There was a vibrant gleaning industry in space exploration. Smaller companies, some being one-man tramps, constantly scanned the data bases, looking for something missed by the larger corporations, or more likely, systems that were not cost-effective for the big boys, but in which a small, low-cost operation could salvage a few BCs.

There was nothing in the last system that would even pique the interest in the gleaners, though. Beth was pretty sure that she was the first and last person to ever travel there.

The green status light started to flash amber, and Beth tensed. She couldn't help it. She'd been through 87 gates in her short 22 years, yet she still had to fight the nervousness that welled up each time before the jump. The gates themselves were essentially foolproof—it was the calculations to enter the gate where a mistake—a fatal mistake—could occur. A vessel could theoretically come apart if it hit the gate off-line, but a more likely accident would be to be sent off to who-knows-where.

Beth would just as soon not experience either one.

The readout reached ten seconds, and time seemed to crawl for her as the remaining seconds ticked off. At three, she gripped the handles alongside her hips and stared ahead at the outside display. Some of her fellow pilots closed their eyes, but Beth wanted to see what was coming—which was a little foolish, because unlike just about every holovid made, there was nothing to see. No stars pulling into lines, no flashing colors. One moment she was in one part of the galaxy, the next she was somewhere else.

The *Lily* passed through the gate and was immediately picked up by Ana on the other side. Within heartbeats, Ana reprogrammed her navigator, took control, and shunted her towards an outbound gate. Still travelling at slightly over the minimum required .54C, it only took her a few seconds to reach her new gate and make the crossing to SG-4021.

Beth would always swear that she could feel a tiny tug as she passed through a gate. Most science-types would scoff at her. It was true that in a very real sense, her body was stretched across the galaxy, her nose lightyears from her butt, but as the saying went, it happened too quickly for her body to realize it was dead and cease functioning.

She took a deep breath, happy to have survived yet again, one of the millions of crossings that would happen today, all without incident. She gave a quick look at her displays. The ship's AI had taken readings the instant the *Lily* had entered the outer system, categorizing stars to confirm her position. This was high-level math, taking into account the ship's supposed position and how long the light from distant stars would take to reach the target system, then comparing that with known star signatures. It was a matter of bracketing, taking a reading, adjusting, and bracketing again until a confirmation was achieved. Despite the computing power of the ship's AI, it took five seconds to confirm that she had reached SG-4021.

The first order of business was, as always, to launch the return gate. Without it, she'd be stuck in the system forever. Even at maximum speed, she didn't have enough food or O2 to make it back to civilization. The *Lily* might eventually make it, centuries or millenniums from now, but she would be a desiccated mummy, far beyond caring.

The AI immediately shifted its scanners to start analyzing the system. A Hummingbird was designed to explore the galaxy, but its scanners were limited. More powerful scanners could easily be put onboard, but the corporate bean-counters stressed weight over anything else. It took more powerful—read *expensive*—engines to get heavier craft up to gate speeds, so every ounce possible was stripped from the exploration scouts. That was why each pilot was in the smallest 2% of humanity. That was why Beth had no real food on the voyage, subsisting on the densely caloric "slime," paste designed to keep a person alive and not much else. That was why the only physical item Beth had been allowed to carry with her was her small silver cross.

The big ships, be they military or corporate, were powered by the terribly expensive FC engines, but those were limited by economies of scale. Smaller craft, such as Beth's Hummingbird, had to make do with the older tech Bradstone engines, and their ability to push craft to gate speeds was a geometric function.

What's that?

The *Lily's* scanners weren't that effective this far out, but they weren't useless. They were picking up something,

something very interesting. The fourth planet from the primary was well within the Goldilocks zone. Her heart jumped

Don't get excited, Floribeth Salinas, she told herself.

There were thousands of planets discovered that fell within the temperature range that supported Earth-type life. Of those, a grand total of 132 had been discovered that either could support human life as is or with minimal terraforming.

Still, the prospect was exciting. There was more to analyze as she shot towards the system's center. An asteroid belt showed promise of valuable metals, and a small inner-planet probably had fissionables, but her attention remained locked on Planet 4 as the *Lily* slowed down. She'd pass by the asteroid belt close enough to confirm the amount and ease of extraction of the metals, but she'd set a course to enter an orbit about the planet so her scanners could make a detailed analysis.

Beth had already sent a confirmation of arrival to HQ, but she hesitated to send anything more yet. Call her superstitious, but she didn't want to jinx herself. Once she knew something for sure, she'd report.

Beth had never been overly superstitious growing up, but five years as a pilot had changed that. The bulk of HB's pilot corps was Filipino, but there were Brazukas, Ukies, Canucks, EnBee's, Canos, Thais, and others, all OPWs, who plied the black for the GTs, and no matter which planet they were from, pilots became superstitious. Her cousin Bobo said it was because deep space was just too vast for the human mind to comprehend, and superstition was merely a way to try and control the uncontrollable.

Beth raised her cross and kissed it.

****

Over the next 26 hours, as the *Lily* passed the outermost planet's orbit and entered the system proper, Beth was focused on her displays. Even this far out, she could tell that the mineral potential in the asteroid belt was significant, more than bonus-worthy. Her dry streak was over, and she'd have a tidy sum to send home. She wanted more, though, and she hoped the beautiful planet four out from the primary would provide that. She already knew it was in the Goldilocks zone, she already knew it had an atmosphere that contained at least some O2. She already knew that the gravity was 1.12 Earth Standard. Those were all well and good, but she had to get the *Lily* in orbit for a more detailed analysis. There were too many possibilities that could render the planet a bust.

Still, Beth spent much of the time daydreaming how she would spend her bonus. She considered, then rejected half-a-dozen ventures. If she was smart about this, she could not only live comfortably for the rest of her life, but live *well*.

She catnapped a few times, drifting off to sleep, but the excitement was too much of a stimulant. There was nothing she could do to affect the outcome, but she was afraid of falling asleep, then waking up to find out she'd been dreaming. She had to speed things up, or she was going to go crazy.

On her current trajectory, the *Lily* would reach SG-4021-4 and slip into orbit in another 32 hours, 13 minutes. The ship was a fairly simple craft, all things considering. Beth had to bleed off her speed, or she'd simply shoot right past the planet, hence the somewhat circuitous route into the system. There was another way, though, that could be taken when the conditions were right. Beth could use the gravity of one of the system's gas giants to slow the ship down—if they were in the correct position relative to each other. As luck would have it, that might be the case.

Beth queried her AI, and the numbers looked good. She could nudge the *Lily* in front of SG-4021-8, gaining a little velocity, but bleeding off more by turning the ship away, letting the planet's gravity act as a drag. This would take some tricky maneuvering—she didn't want to use the planet for the more common gravity assist trajectory, the slingshot which would increase her speed. She'd have to rely on "icing" the *Lily*, swinging its aft end around at full power to push the ship into the right trajectory. She ran the preliminary calculations, and she had a 23-minute window remaining to initiate the change of course.

"How much time will the maneuver save me?"

"Four hours, five minutes, and thirty-two seconds, depending on time of initiation," her AI passed into the implant behind her ear.

That's all? That's not much.

She knew she'd probably be better off taking the standard trajectory in. Deviating from the tried-and-true always introduced a degree of risk. On the other hand, four hours was four hours, and the risk was tiny.

Screw it.

"Initiate new approach," she said.

Immediately, the view on her display shifted as the *Lily* turned to its new course. She zoomed in to SG-4021-8, a large, yellow orb, grimacing for a moment as the image of her little *Lily* getting caught up in the planet's gravity well took over her mind. The chances of that happening were miniscule—something would have to seriously go wrong, but Beth had a tendency of worrying about a worst-case scenario. She adjusted her display, zooming in on SG-4021-4 again. It wasn't the lovely blue of Earth, Society, or any of the water worlds. From this distance, it was a dusky tan, but that was not necessarily a bad sign.

Floribeth, she named the planet, soaking in the sight.

Not that she had naming rights. Some of the early explorers had planets named for them, but in today's universe, the corporations that discovered most of the usable planets decided on the name.

Her route was on her display, and the numbers calculated out. The *Lily* was functioning at peak performance—she might bitch about HB, but they kept the Hummingbirds in top condition. The bottom line was that everything was progressing as planned, and for the first time since her initial readings, Beth began to relax.

The gods of the universe were a fickle bunch, however, and just as Beth's eyes began to flutter closed, her alarm jerked her back to full-alert. She immediately checked life support. A Hummingbird was not very robust, and it was possible that a tiny bit of space flotsam had pierced her repeller field, all the protection her scout ship had. To her relief, the life-support system showed green.

"What's going on?" she queried her AI, checking the output of the engines.

They were operating smoothly. With life support and engines green, pretty much anything else could be handled.

"Foreign object alert."

Beth's heart, which was still racing, slowed down slightly. The AI had the authority to take emergency evasive action to protect the *Lily*, so the mere fact that it hadn't meant whatever it was that had triggered the alert was not an immediate problem. It was probably a swarm of debris in her path. Space was big, and her ship was small, but with enough space rubble along her route, the AI had most likely calculated that the risk of colliding with something her fields couldn't handle had risen from highly unlikely to just unlikely.

She punched up the alert message, figuring that the worse-case scenario would be that she'd have to change course, even reverting back to her original approach. Disappointing, but not really a big deal.

Only, the alert was not for something along her current path. To her surprise, the foreign object alert was for something in the vicinity of SG-4021-4. She scrunched her brows as she considered that.

Planets often had objects around them, from moons to rubble that had been captured over the eons. They tended to be in stable orbits and easy to avoid. Beth wasn't sure why the AI had triggered the alert and was about to query it when she realized that the object's track was not a regular orbit. Whatever was out there was leaving the planet on a separate course.

"What is it?"

"Undetermined."

The *Lily's* scanners were designed to analyze planets, but over broad spectrums. They were not designed to analyze small objects, particularly at this distance.

There was only one thing it could be, she knew: a claimjumper.

HB was the license for the system, she was certain. Their legal team would never make the mistake of letting something like that slip through the cracks. Some tramp explorers poked around the galaxy, trying to find a lode, but they didn't get in the way of the big boys once they'd registered a claim.

"Ping that ship," she told her AI. "And get ready to send back a report."

Beth felt a surge of anger. If Floribeth was, in fact, a Class A planet, she was bound and determined to protect the claim. A simple warning and capture of the claimjumper's engine signature, and whoever was out there would run like a barrio cockroach when the lights came on.

She waited for the response, which she expected would be an apology, then a break for a gate. That confused her for a moment, though. The *Lily* should have picked up the presence of another gate the moment she entered the system.

Were they waiting?

That was stupid. Regulations were sometimes there for a good reason, and even the foolhardiest tramp explorer would drop a gate the moment he or she arrived.

Come to think of it, how did they get here? Through what gate?

For the last 40+ years, all gate coordinates were registered. Sure, a little bribery could open a gate belonging to a planetary government or a smaller corp, and anyone could use a gate—after paying the appropriate fee—once it had been registered, but there was no way HB would let someone through one of their gates before the destination was examined for potential value.

The investigators are going to have a field day with this.

"Ping them again."

"There is no response."

"If they think that staying quiet is going to do them any good . . ." she muttered to herself.

"What kind of ship is it?"

The *Lily's* relatively weak scanners would be more than capable of identifying the ship. All ship engines had a transmitted signature that could be traced. It would be a simple matter of matching the signature with the Directorate database.

"It is not a ship," the AI told her.

"What? Of course, it is. Look at the track."

"I repeat, there is no signature, and scans do not match anything in the database."

"That's impossible. It has to . . ." she started to say before a thought crossed her mind.

Not all century ships, the vast behemoths that first took mankind to the stars, had been accounted for. They'd all been tracked, of course. Anything moving through space collided with tiny particles that then emitted tiny pulses of power, faint, but still there. But the galaxy was huge, and some of the traces of the big ships, which travelled much slower than modern vessels and didn't have the luxury of gates, had simply gotten lost in the noise.

"Could this be a lost colony?" she asked aloud, but more to herself.

If it were, then her bonus would have to be huge. No "lost" colony had been found for a couple of centuries.

"Negative. No century ship could have traveled this far from Earth by this time."

Beth's excitement faded. She really had no idea as to where she was in the galaxy. The *Lily* could flash from one side to the other if the math was correct, but the century ships, without gates, had to traverse the black in the old-fashioned way. Even today, with gate technology, most of the inhabited worlds were in Earth's neighborhood.

So, what the heck is that? she wondered as she watched the track of the object. It was as if it had been flung out of the planet and was now forging its own path.

"Is there volcanic activity on the planet?" she asked.

"Negative."

It had been a long shot, but Beth was wracking her brain for possible answers.

Oh, well, I guess I'll find out soon enough. It looks like our paths are converging.

As soon as the thought had formed, Beth felt a cold chill sweep over her. Space was too big, even within a system, for coincidences like that. If their paths were converging, then there was a reason for that.

That was not a ship . . . at least a ship known to man. It was not a natural phenomenon. As the ancient saying went, "Eliminate the impossible, and what ever remains, no matter how improbable has to be the truth."

"But that's impossible, too," she said aloud.

Unconsciously, her hand reached forward to the mission abort. Push it, and the *Lily* would head back to the gate and the nexus. Her mission would be over. If that really was a Class A world, she'd be giving up her bonus, to be awarded to whoever followed her.

She brought her hand back down. She didn't know what that thing was, so she didn't know if she was in danger. She didn't know if she was safe, either, but the planet was just sitting there, waiting for her, and she wanted it.

"I want full scans on that object," she ordered the AI. "Maintain present course."

She tore her attention away from the object for a moment to check her track. She was already speeding up as the eighth planet pulled at the oblique on her little scout. She'd be icing soon, and the full force of the gas giant's gravity would begin to slow her down. Something about that nagged at her, tickling the back of her mind, but she couldn't grasp it, and in frustration, cleared her mind, dropping an old episode of "The Syntax Gambit" on the display, blocking out the readings, tracks, and everything else. Her AI would let her know if anything changed, and she could lose herself in the opera. She'd seen it ten times if she'd seen it once, and the hopeless love of Jeremy always tugged at her heart.

She tried to lose herself in the story, but for once, she wasn't as deeply invested as she normally was. Her mind kept drifting to Floribeth and the unknown object. She stopped the opera once to go over her SOP, but there weren't any instructions. It was obvious that she should shoot back a message to Ana at HQ, but she didn't know what to tell them that wouldn't make her sound crazy, get recalled, and then lose the bonus to someone else.

She turned back to the show, and just when Meng died, leaving the distraught Jeremy considering suicide, it hit her.

The *Lily* and the object were on a meeting course, but she hadn't performed the icing turn yet. Whatever—whoever—was out there, understood what she was doing, understood that she was coming in and from what direction.

It was impossible, but it was the only explanation. Whatever was out there was coming for her. In her heart, she was sure whoever it was was not meeting her for a civil hello.

If that was a human ship, then by not having an engine signature, by not answering, those in the ship wanted to eliminate her. Beth hoped that was the case. Because if that was not a human ship . . .

It was beyond comprehension. Everyone knew they were alone in the galaxy, at least in so far as a space-going race. It was possible that there was sentient life hidden among the millions of planets, but humans would have detected the signs of movement at speeds, like the swish of bioluminescence that marked the passing of a shark in the oceans of Mother Earth.

If that thing out there was a primitive craft of some sort, native to the planet, then there would be a plethora of signs of the civilization that created it. No, that ship—and Beth knew in her heart that it was a ship—came from outside of the system. It wasn't human.

Shit!

Beth grabbed the manual controls and whipped the *Lily* around, pointing her past the other side of the gas giant looming large in her display. She pushed the power to the max as alarms blared.

"Give me a gravity assist course at max speed to the gate!" she shouted.

Within seconds, a path appeared on her display. She gave the ship a minor correction, and she was hugging the inside of the route. She knew she should turn over the ship to the AI, but she just couldn't release control.

"What's the other ship doing?"

"The unidentified object is adjusting course."

"To where, damn it!"

"Towards SG-4021-8."

Beth felt a surge of hope. The alien ship was still half a system away, and while the *Lily* was only slowly picking up speed, that was a lot of space to make up. With the gas giant's help, her ship was going to make use of a significant burst of speed. She hoped that would keep her far enough in front of the ship to make it to the gate.

She pulled up the alien ship's track. It was accelerating as well, and at a slightly faster rate than the *Lily*.

Beth had a love-hate relationship with her Hummingbird. It was small, barely a floating coffin, and she hated being cooped up in it. But it was also reliable and had returned her from 48 missions so far.

"Make it one more, baby."

The problem with a Hummingbird—or any corporate exploration scout—was that it was made with economy in mind. The costs for a quicker, more maneuverable craft like a Directorate Wasp, were exponentially higher. The corporations didn't care if their OPW pilots spent several days accelerating and then decelerating through gates. And when kilograms mattered, there was nothing to waste in the way of defenses. Corporate scouts were rarely pirated, and it was far cheaper to replace a lost scout and give a nominal payout to the pilot's family than build more robust ships.

Her ship had never let her down, but she'd never been in a race before, and this was one she knew she couldn't afford to lose.

With the first surge of panic subsiding, she turned the *Lily* over to the AI, trusting it to take the quickest, safest pass. Scouts were not made to withstand the pull of something like a gas giant, but the AI would know how close it could take the ship without risk.

For the next 22 minutes, Beth stared at the blip on the screen, only looking away to check her speed. She'd already bled off the bulk of her velocity by the time she'd punched it. A Hummingbird's little engines weren't the most reactive, but the gas giant's gravity had already accelerated the scout far beyond what its engines could do. In a little more than 53 minutes, the *Lily* would start whipping around the planet, gaining even more speed.

The alien ship was gaining, but not fast enough, she thought. Along with the slingshot, and with the *Lily*'s engines screaming, she thought she could reach the gate within 19 hours. She'd know for sure once she broke free from the gas giant's grip.

As she watched the blip on her display, something happened. The blip split in two, one speeding up—quickly.

"What's that?" she asked, her voice breaking.

"Two objects have detached from the primary object. They are accelerating at a high rate of speed."

"Uh . . . how high a rate?" she asked, not really wanting to know the answer.

"Unable to determine using fold scanning."

"Fold" scanners were an important piece of any interstellar craft, from scout to battleship. The *Lily* had an array of inexpensive, but accurate scanners that relied on the visual spectrum. For Floribeth, that meant the scanners were "seeing" the planet almost 50 minutes after the fact due to the speed of light and the distance. The fold scanner, which worked through physics that Beth didn't even try to understand, could "see" things in what was close enough to real time that the lag didn't really matter. Fold scanners didn't show much detail, but the little scout's scanner had been enough to pick up the alien ship—and whatever had detached from the ship and were heading towards her.

"What is their current velocity?"

"Inadequate data input."

"*Guess*, damn it!"

"Approaching .58C."

That shocked Beth. It normally took the *Lily* three days to reach the .54C necessary to pass through a gate, and even at those slow speeds, they would be enough to smush Beth into a red paste without the g-compensators. Whatever was coming her way had to be accelerating at tremendous levels. Nothing alive could survive that.

Could it?

"When will they reach us?"

"Inadequate data input."

Beth started to yell out, but she stopped, took five slow, deliberate breaths, then said, "Make the best possible estimate."

"Fifty-one minutes, thirty seconds, with approximately a one-minute margin of error."

"And when will we pass behind the SG-4021-8?"

"Fifty-five minutes, twenty-two seconds."

Beth's vision started to close in. Whatever was coming her way was going to catch her before she could get the planet between them. She had to goose more speed out of the *Lily*.

She checked her readouts, but the little engine was at maximum output. There was no magic gyvering that could suddenly turn the scout into a fighter.

What about you, big boy? she wondered.

The gas giant loomed large, but her trajectory already had her skirting the very edge of the safe zone. She checked the blips chasing her again—they had already closed the gap significantly.

For all she knew, the blips were a floral delivery service, sent to welcome her to the system. Beth doubted that, though. All she had were two sets of blips, and she thought the two objects that made up the lead blip had malevolent intent. If there was one thing she was sure of, it was that she didn't want to let whatever was represented by those blips catch her.

"Bring the course to here," she said, swiping her finger on the display to indicate a new course.

"Negative. That course is not within accepted safety parameters."

"Neither is getting an interstellar missile up our butts. Do it."

"Negative. I am not authorized to allow you to put Hamdani Brothers property in jeopardy."

Beth wanted to scream in frustration. The *Lily's* AI, like everything else on the ship, was a basic model, adequate to do the job, but not much else. It was nothing like higher capability AIs that had simulated personalities and could function more like humans.

Beth was not going to sit there and argue with a bunch of silicate cells when their very survival was at risk. She didn't even hesitate. Flipping up the cover near her right hand, she hit the switch.

Immediately, the ship's AI went dead. The ship still functioned as a basic numbers cruncher, and it would keep the ship operating, but it no longer had the independent capacity that made it an AI. That part of its silicate circuits had just been fried. Beth took control of the *Lily* and swung it on a closer line to the planet.

She almost expected to feel a surge as the gravity pull got stronger, but that was ridiculous. The *Lily* was going through heavy acceleration even without the change in course, and her g-compensators, well, compensated.

Beth didn't think the change in course would speed her up significantly, but what it did was shorten her distance to travel until she was behind the big planet. She hoped that would be enough.

The planet grew larger and larger, and twice, Beth had to zoom out on her display. All the time, the leading blip, which had now split into two separate blips, closed the distance. She kept running the calculations, and as the alien torpedoes, as she was now calling them, came closer, the calculations became more accurate. It soon became apparent that her change of course was not enough. She was going to get caught a minute too soon.

"They can probably follow me around the planet, anyway," she muttered.

She nudged the course over, closer to the planet, so that she would pass right alongside the exosphere. Alarms blared, but mercifully, the AI didn't say a word.

"This is it," she told herself as she reached the planet.

Outside, immense forces were pulling at the *Lily*, something it was not designed to take. It even shuddered, something Beth had never felt before. Beth almost panicked, knowing she'd hit the limits of the exosphere, and she was afraid she'd bounce off, exposing the ship to the torpedoes that were on her ass. With a firm hand, she steadied the scout, wishing now that she could turn it back over to the slagged AI.

The first torpedo materialized on the visuals. Long and cylindrical, it did look like a torpedo. Beth was tempted to close her eyes, but if she was going to die, she wanted to see it coming.

But it didn't come. It started to slow down. The *Lily* shuddered more violently, and something broke free to lodge beneath her right foot, but on the display, the first torpedo began to yaw. Suddenly, it swerved and dove into the planet, as the *Lily* began to whip around the gas giant.

Where's the second one? Where is it?

The gas giant was big—huge, in fact. But the *Lily* was moving very fast. Within moments, the ship slingshotted around and broke free of the planet's grip, heading back out into space. Beth kept it on course to reach the gate, but she ran every scanner she had back toward the planet, looking for the second torpedo. It never appeared.

Somehow, by some miracle, she had shaken the alien craft, and the *Lily* was still intact. She pulled out her cross and kissed it.

Beth switched the fold scanner to the remaining blip, the one still far behind. It was still accelerating, but with the gas giant's assist, Beth had opened up the distance. It had shifted course as well, moving to an intercept that steered clear of SG-4021-8.

Beth ran several scenarios. She wished she could turn the AI back on, but disabling it was a safety option, in case an AI went rogue (which was an extremely rare occurrence). As such, it would take a tech to install a new AI. Still, even with out the AI making the calculations, it became obvious that unless the ship chasing her had something else up its sleeve, the *Lily* should enter the gate with around 40 minutes to spare. She was still nervous about another set of torpedoes, but after an hour without any more being fired, she began to relax. She even fell asleep for two hours.

Eighteen hours, twelve minutes, and fifteen seconds after slingshotting around the gas giant, Pilot Two Floribeth Salinas O'Shea Dalisay, Hamdani Exploration Corps passed through the gate. As per regulations in existence since the formation of the Directorate, but never followed, as far as she knew, she triggered the self-destruct, and the gates to and from SG-4021 were reduced to their component atoms.

Chapter 2

Beth was whisked down the corridors, two rather large, imposing men one step behind her. She wasn't a prisoner, but the two goons left her little doubt that they would take her by force should she try to leave.

Within seconds of destroying the gate, the *Lily* had been locked down. The gates were the lifeblood of humankind, and they were sometimes attacked by anarchists, but she was a vetted pilot, not some crazy anarchist with a bone to pick. And it wasn't as if they were difficult to replace. The gate itself was almost inconsequential: a powersource and a projection field. Gates such as the one Beth had emplaced outside the SG-4021 system, which relied on solar power, massed less than a kilogram. It was the programming that was the difficult aspect of creating them, requiring something along the lines of an Ana to make them functional. HB could replace the one Beth had destroyed in a few hours, if they wanted.

Which they couldn't possibly want to do. Not now. But other than her first report, given from inside the *Lily*, Beth hadn't spoken to anyone. Ana had taken over the *Lily*'s controls and brought her in to HQ, but Beth had been in a comms blackout.

She'd been met at the dock by the two goons, OPWs like her, but whereas she'd been hired due to her diminutive size, these two were chosen for the opposite physical attributes. They were huge!

Technically, she didn't have to go with the two guards. HB would have to formalize custody for that to happen. But the company could fire her on a whim, and she valued her job. Once her report made it up the chain, this would all be cleared up. She should even receive a company commendation—and hopefully, the bonus for the asteroid belt she'd left behind.

Beth was a little peeved that she hadn't been met by the corporate brass. The fact that there were aliens in the system, space-faring aliens, no less, would reverberate through humanity, and she not only found them, but kept them from using the gate.

Well, she didn't know if they could actually *use* it, but a human ship could follow the trail of another without the actual calculations, so why couldn't an alien ship?

She'd followed the regulations and destroyed the gate. Let the Directorate open another one with the might of the Navy behind it. Let them work out a first contact.

Second contact. They tried to blow me up on the first.

Beth might have just saved humanity from an alien invasion, and she wasn't being treated like a hero. It was starting to get on her nerves as she trooped down the passage.

The trio stopped at a non-descript door. The first goon leaned in, had his retina read, and it opened with a slight hiss. Inside the room was a simple table with a single chair on one side, three on the other. Just like in a police holovid. Goon 1 held out a hand and indicated that she take a seat.

"You can speak, you know," she said as she sat down.

He didn't reply.

With a shrug, Beth sat. She was running on adrenaline, hyped by what had transpired. This was big—very big. She understood that HB, the Directorate, and probably the Corporate Council would want to determine how to break the news to the public. She might be kept under wraps while this was worked out, sworn to silence. She didn't understand, however, why she wasn't already speaking with the HB brass—the local bosses in person, and even the CEO back on Earth. Surely, they'd be all over this.

There was an old-fashioned-but-now-back-in-fashion analog clock on the wall. Beth sat and watched the second hand slowly make its circuits around and around. It was mesmerizing, in a way, and Beth felt herself calm down. She might have just made one of the biggest discoveries in history, but she was just a tiny asterisk among the trillions of humans. The news itself was the big thing. She knew she was being a little bit juvenile in thinking that all the big wigs would be running over to assuage her ego when things had to be in chaos now.

Still, it wouldn't hurt to have someone come and ask for my debrief.

"Right, guys?" she asked, just like that and not giving them a reference.

Neither said a word.

Almost twenty minutes had passed before the door whispered open and a harried-looking man came in, p-link in hand. He hadn't had the full mods of a GT, but it had been obvious that he'd had some sculpting done. His face was just too perfect, almost elfin with the lilac eyes that were all the rage now. If Beth had to guess, she'd say he'd been an OPW like her, but one who'd risen in the ranks, making enough money for his mods. He sat down across from her and studied his p-link for a moment.

About time, Beth thought, leaning forward in anticipation of telling the man just what had happened.

He finally looked up and said, "Pilot Two Dalisay, I'm Accountant Eight Huhn."

That took Beth by surprise. *An accountant? Why am I being debriefed by an accountant?*

As a level eight, he was in upper management. There were probably only a few senior accountants in the entire Nexus Prime facility. But what did she have to say to a bean-counter?

"Can you please tell me why you destroyed both your AI and the gate pair to SG-4021?" he asked without preamble.

Beth stared at him in shock, her mouth dropping open.

"Well, I'd appreciate an answer, Pilot," he said in the same even voice.

"Because . . . because I was being pursued by an alien ship that was trying to kill me!"

The goon standing behind the accountant broke his stern visage, raising an eyebrow before recovering to his stone face. The accountant sniffed dismissively.

"So you reported."

What? What's he getting at?

"Yes, I reported. That's what happened. I destroyed the gate pair because of the Directorate regulations."

"Yes, IR 2.09.01. I am familiar with it. It's something no one has ever done before, however."

"That's because no one has ever run into aliens before," Beth said with a raised voice, standing up.

The goon behind Huhn took a step forward, but with a roll of his eyes, the accountant raised a hand in a casual dismissal. Beth might be a third of the accountant's weight, but that flick of the hand infuriated her. She swallowed her anger and sat back down. He might be a dick, but he was an executive level eight, and someone in her position didn't make it a habit of getting on someone that high's bad side.

"I'm sorry, sir. To make it clear, I encountered and alien ship that fired upon me. I returned to Nexus Prime, and as per Directive regulation IR two-point, uh . . ."

"Two-point-zero-nine-point-zero-one," he prompted.

That made her angrier, but she bit back a retort, then said, "Thank you, sir. Yes, that regulation. I destroyed the gate pair to isolate the SG-4021 system from Nexus Prime."

"Assuming for a moment that I believe you, which I do not, why did you null your AI?"

"I had to. The enemy torpedoes would have hit me unless I hugged the exosphere, and the AI would not allow that. If I hadn't, I wouldn't be alive and here now."

"So, somehow, a human pilot was better able to fly a Hummingbird than the best AI HB can offer?"

"Yes, sir. As I said, I had to push the envelope in order to survive. I *had* to do it."

"So, you nulled the AI, the only entity that could verify the existence of this so-called alien ship? How convenient."

For the second time within a minute, Beth just stared at the man, mouth hanging open, before she was able to sputter out, "Just pull the ship's record! You'll see it."

He looked at her scornfully and said, "And how do you expect us to do that? You nulled your AI."

"Yes, I did. I told you why. But can't one of our tech teams recover that?"

"Please, Pilot Dalisay, you give us more credit that we deserve. That, or you don't give the techs who designed the null enough credit. When you decided to null the AI, you wiped it clean. That's why we call it 'nulling.' It cannot be recovered.

"So, once again, what proof do you have that you encountered an *alien*, Pilot?"

Beth simply looked at him, uncertain what to say. It was news to her that a nulled AI could not be recovered—if that was even true. Criminals always tried to wipe their p-links, but no matter what new method they used, the police were always able to recover the data.

"I thought so, Pilot. What we do know, however, is that the mineral wealth in the system is significant." He paused a moment, for all the world looking like a cat about to pounce on a mouse. "And SG-4021-4 has every indication that it could possibly be a Class A world."

"Yes, sir, I know that. I shot back updates on my findings."

"Did you mean to do that?"

"Sir?"

"Perhaps as you got closer, you confirmed that SG-4021-4 was in fact a Class A planet."

"I was hoping, but nothing was confirmed yet," she told him, wary of where this was leading.

"So, you say. But what if you did receive confirmation that it was, in fact, a Class A planet, then decided to shop around that information?"

It took a moment for Beth to understand what he was saying, but once she did, righteous indignation set in.

I almost got killed on this mission and brought back astounding news, and I get this shit?

"It makes sense that you would null your AI, then concoct a reason why we shouldn't go back to the system."

"I assure you, sir, that everything I've reported is the truth," Beth said through clenched lips, trying to remain civil.

"Your word, without anything to back it up.

"Let me tell you what's going to happen, Pilot Dalisay. First, we're docking your pay to cover the cost of both the gates and the AI. I've already totaled the amount, and that will run you 567,446 BC," he said with a sneer.

Bullshit. There's no way they cost that much. And so nice of you to have it down to a specific BC.

"And before you ask, no, you aren't fired. You're still under contract, confined to your quarters until we get to the bottom of this. Once we evaluate the system and have proof of your perfidy, we'll remand you to custody."

For the first time since Huhn arrived, Beth realized that she was in big trouble. If HB fired her, she'd be technically free to go. HB could sue her for damages, but they'd have a difficult time collecting such an exorbitant fine. You can't milk a dry cow, after all. By keeping her under contract, she'd be working decades to pay off the fine.

It wasn't as if she could break the contract herself. Workers didn't have that right—only the corporations did. And by keeping her under contract, if they could show financial damage, then they would have the legal right to confine her in the HB prison.

"And if you go to SG-4021 and find out I am telling the truth?" she asked, unable to keep the anger out of her voice.

Accountant 8 Huhn laughed, which made her angrier. "If you are telling the truth, well, you still owe the replacement costs, so good luck with that.

"Now, I'm just here to present you the bill. Security Six Onswalt will be here momentarily. You can tell your tale to her and see if she believes you."

Which wasn't going to happen, Beth knew. Sec6 Onswalt had been an OPW from Tychee, and she'd climbed the ladder into employee status by being the biggest asshole in the company. She came from the same roots as all the rest of the OPWs, but she seemed to resent their presence, and took every opportunity to slap them down.

The door hissed open, and Huhn said, "Speaking of her—" before he stood up, hitting his chin on his chest and saying, "Mzee Teneriffe, how can I help you?"

Beth felt a surge of hope, and she stood as well, turning and chinning. Mzee Teneriffe was an anomaly, a GT who not only had a job, but one protecting the powerless. She was the Directorate rep for workers' rights. Tall and slender, as all GTs were, she had chosen a light-rose skin color, and her silver hair, almost metallic in appearance, never had even a strand out of place. She looked the part of a typical GT, but unlike most of her kind, she seemed to genuinely care for the OPWs and general employees.

"What can you do for me, Accountant Eight Huhn? I should think that would be obvious," she said, a measure of icy steel in her lilting voice.

"I'm afraid I don't, Mzee."

"Hmm. You seem to have Pilot Two Dalisay under arrest, and I have not been informed of this."

"I must beg to respectfully disagree, Mzee. The Pilot—" Beth could almost hear the disdain in his voice when he said her title, "is merely being debriefed on her last mission."

The Mzee gave a pointed look at the two guards, one after the other. They both averted their eyes.

"They are only here to protect Pilot Two Dalisay," he said, grasping for words.

"I didn't realize that the halls here in HB headquarters were that dangerous for your pilots. Has there been an incident here, like on Warm Heart?"

Beth almost smiled as Huhn blanched, his dark skin almost turning grey. Three years ago, the local population had risen up, demanding the removal of all OPWs. Twenty-three EnBee OPWs were killed in the rioting, and Wei Min Industries was fined twenty-million BCs.

"No, Mzee, nothing like that," he stammered out.

"Good. Then I will assume that, as you have not levied charges against Pilot Dalisay and there is no threat to her well-being, she is free to come with me now."

Huhn looked up at one of the guards, and the man shifted his gaze to the ceiling. The accountant wasn't going to get any help there.

"Uh . . . no, Mzee Teneriffe. As soon as Security Six Onswalt is finished with her, she is free to go with you."

"I used the word 'now,' if you have ears with which to hear," Accountant Eight Huhn," she said, and then turning to Beth, added, "Do you want to come with me, Pilot?"

Beth glanced at Huhn, who was staring daggers at her. She knew she should stay. The Mzee had no real authority here. True, she could cause problems for the company. But if she did, the company would most likely take it out on Beth.

Screw it, Beth told herself.

"Yes, Mzee, I would like that."

"Then come with me . . . unless you have an objection, Accountant Eight?"

"I . . . I will bring this matter up with Mzee Gossamer," he said.

"I'm sure you will."

Mzee Gossamer was the Operations Officer for HB at their Nexus Prime facility. He had direct control over every person in the organization, answerable only to the CEO, Mzee One Off. Beth's heart fell when she heard Huhn's words. Except for meeting Mzee Teneriffe a couple of times, she avoided the few GTs at Nexus Prime. Nothing good came from attracting their attention.

Mzee Teneriffe gestured for the door, and with an air of nonchalance that she didn't feel, she preceded her out into the hallway.

"OK, Pilot Dalisay," she said once the door closed behind them, "you're in a heap of trouble. You'd better have a good reason for destroying those gates, or there won't be anything I can do to help you."

Chapter 3

"You got the next one?" Bill asked.

"Don't you have reports to do or something?"

"Fuck them," Bill said.

Beth rolled her eyes, then said, "Play Episode Six."

Her stage flickered, and the same ad they'd seen before watching the last two episodes urging them to pre-order Season Four appeared.

"Good of them to tease us with that," Bill said as Horti and Caleb ran together through a spectacular desert scene, firing their blasters over their shoulders at an unseen enemy.

Season Three was turning out to be pretty good. With the Dayson Empire and the League of Restraint going at each other, no one knew to which side the fledgling Justice Navy would pledge allegiance. The trailer for next season wasn't leaving any clues.

The Justice Navy was a favorite among pilots and crew throughout human space. It was pure opera—capital ships were not anywhere near as maneuverable as on the holovid, nor did they fight battles within close visual range, passing each other like medieval knights jousting on horseback. The Q-fighters, which both Horti and Caleb flew, had only a passing resemblance to real life. Still, the series was popular.

Bill was Lead Pilot Bill Barker, a Canuck OPW, and as such, a rarity. Not many Canucks were small enough for Hummingbirds, but he'd been with HB for almost fifteen years, rising to be the senior pilot, or "kapo," at Nexus Prime. A kapo was the practical leader of an OPW team, be they pilots, cooks, or guards, handing out assignments and acting as the liaison between the OPWs and the company staff. Bill hated the term kapo, which went back centuries and referred to a prisoner who guarded other prisoners, so the rest of the pilots delighted in calling him that at every opportunity.

As kapo, he had reports to submit at 0700 and 1800 each day. It was now 1647, and each episode of *The Justice Navy* ran an hour. As far as Beth knew, Bill hadn't started his reports, and he'd be cutting it close.

Not her call, however. She was glad he was there with her, though. Since returning to Nexus Prime, she wasn't exactly confined to her quarters, but Personnel Administrator Six Martinez, who was in charge of all OPWs in Nexus Prime, had recommended that she stay in her quarters, out of sight if not out of mind. So, for five days and counting, she'd only left her small quarters to go to the chow hall and the head. Despite having an almost unlimited library of holovids and books, she was going stir-crazy, so when Bill had shown up, she'd scooted over to give him space on her rack, and they'd watched two episodes of *The Justice Navy* together.

Bill wasn't bad company—for a kapo.

The ad for Season Four mercifully ended, and Episode Six started. Horti was at a crossroads. Dalia and Caleb were battling for her affections, but she liked both of them as just friends. Beth settled in to watch, but her mind, numbed by hours of holovids, started drifting.

She'd been debriefed three times now—luckily never by Sec6 Onswalt. The first time, both Mzee Teneriffe and PA6 Martinez had been present. The next two times, only Martinez was there, which had made her nervous. None of the three debriefs were nearly as confrontational as her meeting with Huhn, but they hadn't gone well either, as far as she was concerned. No one acted like they believed her account, and now she was beginning to doubt herself.

Was it possible that it had all been a hallucination? Everything had been so vivid in her mind, and she'd been so sure of herself. Now, she wasn't feeling so sure.

Beth had been screened a million ways from Sunday before becoming a pilot. Being isolated in a tiny Hummingbird for days on end required a stable mind and a strong sense of self. She had that stamp of approval, and she didn't feel crazy. But then again, as Bobo had said yesterday when she broached her fears to him, crazy people always thought they were the sane ones. Bobo was her cousin, and she loved him, but he could be a pain in the ass.

"Ha, I knew it!" Bill said, elbowing Beth in the ribs.

"What?" she asked, turning her thoughts back to the show.

"Dalia! I told you she was no good."

Over Beth's stage, Dalia was slipping a tiny message capsule under a park bench, the standard spy trope. Beth raised her eyebrows in surprise. She hadn't expected her to turn out to be a bad guy. Bill had said she was bad, but he'd also said she was a good guy, too, vacillating between the two statements, so there was no way she was going to give him credit for that.

Dalia LeMorde was madly in love with Horti, and the general chatter in the undernet was that she was going to win over Horti's heart. Beth thought that was more hope than anything else. Dalia, with her pale white complexion and black hair, and Horti, with her ebony skin and white hair, were both smoking hot, and *The Justice Navy* was pretty liberal with sexing up the scenes. Pirate digi-artists had already created sex scenes between the two that could be downloaded from the dark net, but people wanted the real thing.

Hah, "real thing." Even the official show isn't "real."

After a retro-revival of using real actors, most of the studios had reverted back to the tried-and-true digital 3D constructs for their shows. Horti, the heartthrob of men and women throughout the galaxy, was merely a construct of electrons. Not that it mattered to her millions of fans. They loved her.

"Give me a Coke, OK?" she asked Bill.

With both of them squeezed into her rack to watch the show, she was up against the bulkhead, and he was between her and the therma.

"Pause the show, at least," he grumbled, reaching below the bed to pull out a Coke packet.

Her stage was set to her voice, so she said, "Pause," while he popped the packet into the therma, checked the setting, and pushed start. Ten seconds later, the therma dinged, and he reached in, pulled out the now-cold packet, and passed it over to her.

"OK, Your Highness. If you can start it up again?"

Beth took a long sip, making a show of it before saying, "Resume."

Almost all pilots had a food or drink weakness, which they called *kanoom*. Long days of eating slime and drinking recycled urine created cravings. For Beth, it was the old standby, Coke. It might have been developed in the days before space flight, but it was the perfect foil for rejuvenating dulled taste buds.

Bill's *kanoom* was a Lemon Sun, the child's candy, and he constantly sucked on one when he wasn't plying the black. At least that was the only time he was supposed to suck on them. Everyone was sure that he snuck a few with him on each mission. Beth was jealous of that. If she could smuggle a Coke onboard the *Lily*, she would.

She took another long sip, then shifted her focus back on the show when her hatch light lit, accompanied by a soft chime.

"No room for anyone else in here," Bill yelled, which was not exactly true—someone could sit on the deck and watch—and didn't make much sense, as the quarters were soundproofed. No one outside could hear him shouting.

"I think it might be Iris," Beth said to Bill's groan before she said, "Open."

But it wasn't their fellow pilot who entered. Mzee Teneriffe stooped to stick her head into the small stateroom. Both pilots scrambled out of the rack to stand facing her. It wasn't just her. Behind the Directorate rep, another GT stood, looking inside. Tall, like all GTs, his skin was a bright purple, which immediately labeled him a stranger. There weren't any purple-skinned GTs in the entire HB facilities in Nexus Prime, at least not until now.

"May I have a moment of your time, Pilot Dalisay?" the Mzee asked.

"Yes, Mzee. Of course," Beth said.

The GT made a show of looking around the small stateroom, then shrugged.

"Oh, yes, sorry. We can go wherever you want," Beth said, blushing in embarrassment.

All of the pilot staterooms were small, as befitted their stature. They were much, much better accommodations than most OPWs would ever see—as a housekeeper, Beth had shared a dormitory with 31 other women—but it was way too small for a GT to come inside.

"Excuse me, Mzee," she said, turning to Bill and asking, "Do you want to stay here?"

He took a long look up at the GT, then at the GT hovering outside in the passage. Bill could be protective of the rest of the pilots, and he was undoubtedly wondering what was going on and what he could do about it. Teneriffe was a "good" GT, but she was still a GT.

"I'll wait here, if you don't mind, until you get back."

"Granting Senior Pilot Barker quarters control, Level 1, ninety minutes," she said.

With Level 1, he could leave her quarters or control her stage, if he wanted, for the next hour-and-a-half. He nodded, but she could see this was gnawing at him.

Beth stepped out, and Mzee Teneriffe straightened back up with what looked like relief on her face. Behind her, the purple GT stood waiting. No, not exactly purple. As she moved, Beth could see the GT's purple shift to a yellow and back to purple under the even illumination of the station's lighting. That had to be a very expensive genmod, even for a GT. This was a very important person, she realized.

She was so caught up with the new GT that she didn't notice the norm with them until the woman said, "If you'll come with us, Mzee Patel-Anand would like to ask you some questions."

Beth quickly looked up at Mzee Teneriffe, but the GT didn't look concerned. The way the woman had said that it was the purple GT who wanted to talk to her let her know that he was running this, and that meant Teneriffe was only there as a courtesy. It was taken as gospel that norms, especially those in the lower social strata like OPWs, did not talk to strange GTs. Nothing good usually came from it.

With the norm herding her like a lost duckling, Beth made her way down the passage, trying to look unconcerned. She passed Waldemeier and Absinthe, who were going in the opposite directions, but they hugged the bulkheads, mouths hung open as the four of them passed. Beth smiled and gave her two fellow pilots a wink, projecting a confidence that she didn't feel.

The norm, who had not introduced herself yet, scanned her eye into a carriage door, which whispered open. Beth was almost disappointed that it looked exactly like the carriages that transported low-level workers around the station. She wasn't sure what she'd expected, but something a little grander, at least. The norm took a physical key, held it to the reader, and Q-12 appeared on the readout.

Beth shrugged. To her, all the executive levels were one and the same, and since she didn't know the layout of the—

Wait. The Q Deck? That's the Directorate deck!

This station was owned by the Hamdani Brothers, but as with all large stations, a space was reserved for the Directorate, where they and only they held sway. Beth only knew what she'd gleaned from various holovids, so she didn't know if that was completely accurate, but the idea was that the Directorate levels were sovereign territory, much like the embassies on the Earth of old.

The carriage whisked the four along the gerbil tubes and came to a stop, the door opening. The norm stepped out, followed by Beth and the two GTs. Beth had never been in Directorate territory, and she wasn't disappointed. While the carriage had been nothing out of the ordinary, it was immediately obvious that this deck was far from standard, starting with the deck itself, which instead of the hard tiles she was used to, had a slightly giving surface. Beth's light weight didn't do much to compress the flooring, but she could feel the difference.

The lighting was different as well. The station's lights were a low glow into the white wavelengths. In this deck, the light had more of a yellow tint, more like sunlight. The two GTs started off down the passage, and Beth stopped dead.

Under this deck's lighting, the purple GT's skin shifted back and forth with greater saturation, the yellow almost flowing in waves across his skin as his body moved.

"He's beautiful, isn't he?" the norm whispered to her. "Just arrived yesterday. But come on, we don't want to keep him waiting."

He *was* beautiful, his skin vibrant, and the deference most low-end normals had for the Golden Tribe kicked in. She felt an urge to serve the man, to do what he wanted. The days were long gone when the GT were actually golden. For a century, the rich and powerful underwent the inordinately expensive genmod, becoming taller, stronger, and with their signature golden skin. At the same time, they consolidated their hold on the economy, becoming the de facto rulers of mankind. Ninety years ago, Mzee T'Symba broke with tradition, using a different program that gave her a sky-blue skin with whiter-than-white hair. Initially shunned by the other GTs, she became a cultural phenomenon among the norms, and soon, while all GTs kept the tall, slender bodies, skin choices became individual signatures. Beth had never seen the purple-and-yellow shifting skin that Mzee Patel-Anand sported, however. If it was a new program, it had to be extremely expensive, which meant that this GT was someone very, very important.

At 4' 6", Beth was half of Mzee Patel-Anand's height, and she felt more than a little self-conscious as she followed him past paneled walls and art that looked expensive to her untrained eye. There'd been times as a small child that she'd dreamed of undergoing genmod, to become one of the "beautiful people," but folks in her social status almost never rose that far. Even wealthier norms rarely underwent the process. It had to be done before a GT entered puberty, and most norms who amassed the wealth necessary did so well into their adulthood. They might pay for sculpting, but that was not the same thing.

Even if she'd been born with the money, Beth doubted she'd have gone through the process. It was reportedly an extremely painful procedure with a 4% mortality rate. Neither of those facts appealed to her. More pertinently, as Beth had matured, she'd become very comfortable with her body and looks, perhaps even a slightly bit vain. She was happy with who she was.

Still, Mzee Patel-Anand looked like a god.

The GT turned into an office, followed by Mzee Teneriffe, Beth, and the other normal. Beth's eyebrows rose in surprise. She was not being escorted into an interrogation room, but rather a lush office, complete with a huge desk and comfortable-looking furniture. The main focus of the office was an entire glass wall, exposed to space. She'd seen wall displays that beamed an image of space to an inner wall, but she had the suspicion that this was the real thing. As a pilot, she was used to the sight, but for an office and a station . . . well, this was one more piece of data, as if she needed it, to prove that she wasn't in Kansas anymore. She was swimming in deep ocean waters now.

The norm pointed to one of the couches, and Beth took a seat. They were made for GT sizes, not Hummingbird pilots. She sat back, her feet poking out in front of her, not reaching the deck, as if she was a small child playing grownup.

"Annabelle, could you get us some drinks, please?" Mzee Patel-Anand asked. "I believe Pilot Dalisay would like a Coke?"

Beth just nodded as the other norm, Annabelle, walked over to a shiny copper tender on the credenza. The tender probably cost more than Beth could make in a couple of years, but her attention was focused on the GT. He'd known what she liked to drink. It was no secret, and anyone with access to company records could find that out. He wasn't company, not that it would be an issue, but the fact that he, a GT, had bothered to find out what a lowly OPW pilot drank had ramifications she couldn't quite grasp. She couldn't help but wonder if he was making her relax all the better to lead her into a trap.

The tender hummed loudly, causing Beth to jump, but it was only preparing an espresso. None of the three said a word, and Beth kept her eyes on the window-wall, which seemed to be a safer option than staring at either of the two GTs. She could see a bright star which had to be one of the other stations in Nexus Prime—probably New Horizons, if she had to guess. To her relief, Annabelle returned with a tray, handing Mzee Patel-Anand a white cup of something, Mzee Teneriffe the espresso, and Beth her Coke. Beth shifted her focus from space to the Coke, as if it was uber-interesting and not like every other Coke she'd ever drunk. Annabelle sat down as well, sipping a mug that steamed slightly.

Mzee Patel-Anand took a long, slurping sip of his drink and sighed, which piqued Beth's curiosity. Despite herself, she looked up and caught his eye.

"Good Styx Nectar," he said, raising his cup in a half-toast when he saw her looking at him.

Beth dropped her eyes back to her Coke. She'd never even heard of Styx Nectar, and by looking up at him, she'd broken one of the unwritten rules. People in her position never initiated contact with a GT.

Water under the bridge, I guess. I'm already right in his crosshairs.

"Thank you for agreeing to meet with me, Pilot Dalisay," the GT said, putting his cup on the low table between them.

Not that I had a choice.

"I'm here for a short time, so if you don't mind, I'm going to skip the pleasantries and get to the point. If you don't mind, would you please give me your account of what happened at SG-4021. Please don't leave out anything, no matter how insignificant you think it to be."

Beth almost shook her head, stopping herself just in time. She'd known this had to be related to the mission.

Nothing else she'd ever done in her entire life could possibly interest a GT. So now, even a Directorate GT was going to convince her she experienced nothing? She was already doubting her memories, and this would be just one more nail in the coffin.

"I've already been debriefed several times, Mzee. Those are all in the company record now," she said, squirming uncomfortably in her seat.

"I've seen those, but I'd like you to go through it again. Tell me what you saw, what you thought."

His tone was calm and collected, but there was that underlying steel in his voice that created a compulsion to obey. It wasn't for nothing the GTs had risen to their current position in humankind.

With a mental sigh, Beth began to recount what she remembered. She spoke softly, almost in a monotone, and the GT simply sat there and listened. Annabelle whispered into her throat mic a few times as Beth spoke, but Beth couldn't understand what she'd said to provoke her to take notes at that specific moment.

Beth didn't know how far she should continue, so she was relieved when Mzee Patel-Amand lifted his outstretched hand, palm up, to stop her. She waited for the inevitable.

"That explains the question Javier had about the jump in the Q-readings," he said, looking to Teneriffe. "Annabelle, get our transport back to Sahra and set up a meeting with the principles."

Annabelle nodded, stood, and left the room. Patel-Amand leaned over and quietly said something to Teneriffe that Beth didn't catch.

What now?

The GT turned his attention back to Beth and said, "Thank you, Pilot Dalisay, for your time. You've been most helpful clearing up a few items. A first-hand account can always fill in some of the blanks."

Beth was confused. She looked up at him and tried to digest his words.

"You mean . . . you believe me? About what happened?"

Now it was Mzee Patel-Amand's turn to look confused, his perfect purple brows scrunched together. "Why wouldn't I believe you? You were telling me the truth, weren't you?"

"I mean . . . I mean, no one with the company believes me. They said I made it all up, then wiped my AI to cover my tracks."

He smiled, then said, "Your AI's data confirms what you've told me."

"But I was told that once you null an AI, whatever was in there is lost forever."

Both GTs laughed aloud at that, looking at each other with "oh, isn't she cute?" expressions on their faces.

"Rest assured, Pilot Dalisay, that the Directorate has methods to recover anything. Even without your ship's records, there was enough picked up through the gate to corroborate the report you gave. No, I do believe what happened to you. I also believe that the most likely explanation is the one you presented, that you made contact with an alien race."

Beth's mouth gaped open, and she tried to speak, but nothing came out. She'd been so sure of the facts after returning to Nexus Prime, only to have the constant rebuttals make her doubt her own memories. To have those same memories accepted by the Directorate was a welcome relief.

I'm not crazy!

"We've been expecting this for some time now, but the fact is that you were the one who made history. Annabelle will brief you before we leave, but the gist of it is that you're going to have to remain quiet for some time still. Can I count on you for that?"

At the moment, she was so relieved that she would have promised him her first-born child, so she said, "Yes, Mzee. Of course."

"I knew that. You've got an exemplary record, especially from someone of your background."

Beth was almost militantly proud of New Cebu and her people, but she let his condescending attitude slide.

"This will only be temporary. Just understand that at some point your name will be known."

Beth had hoped for recognition when she reached Nexus Prime, but that had faded after the reception she'd received. She might feel differently in the future, but for the moment, she was just happy that she'd been vindicated.

And I'm not crazy!

Chapter 4

"You're looking happy," Bill said, sliding down into the seat across from her.

"I thought you were going out?" Beth asked, wiping the tolly sauce from her lips.

"I was. I was already in the bay when it got cancelled. Something beyond the company. Probably forgot to register the license, if you ask me."

Beth felt a pang of undeserved guilt. Could the Directorate have closed off the sector, and had Bill been given a destination to that same sector? The galaxy was vast, but it made sense that HB was exploring sector by sector.

"Probably would have been a dry well, anyway," she said. "Get some chow. The Vargas Fingers are pretty good."

"Yeah, I can see the sauce all over your mouth. And shirt."

Beth looked down, then reached with her finger to wipe the glob of white sauce off her left breast. She put the finger in her mouth, sucking the it clean.

"Too good to waste, huh?"

Bill just rolled his eyes. He was happily—and monogamously—married, and some of the pilots like to flirt with him, knowing he wouldn't do anything about it. Beth shied away from that kind of thing, but she was feeling too good at the moment, and she had to act out.

I'm not crazy, she told herself for the umpteenth time.

"What else they got?" Bill asked, looking over to the chow line.

"Chops, I think. With apples."

He wrinkled his lips, then said, "I'll hit the autochef."

"You usually do," Beth said with a shrug.

Chow on the station was generally good, even on the lower decks. There were always two main courses cooked by the staff, and since many of the cooks were OPWs from New Cebu, those often included Filipino dishes. If neither of the two main courses tickled the diner's fancy, they could dial up any of 200+ dishes from the autochefs in the corner.

Bill came back a few minutes later with a cheeseburger.

"Glad you're expanding your culinary horizons," she told him.

"Hey, I like burgers. And I had Pasta Ricci yesterday, so there!"

"Ooh, pushing the envelope, Herr Kapo. Real adventurous."

"Eat me," he said, taking a big bite out of his burger.

"Nah, I'll stick with my Vargas Fingers."

She saw Absinthe and waved her over. The Brazuka had a plate of the plain chops with a fresh salad. Absinthe was just as short as Beth, but a lot curvier, and that caused problems with her weight. No Vargas Fingers with tolly sauce for her. She looked wistfully at Beth's plate for a moment before sitting down.

"You still under house arrest?" she asked.

"Never was."

"Right, that's why you've been holed up in your room all this time."

Beth shrugged, saying nothing. She took another bite of her food.

"Well?"

"Well, what?"

"Well fucking what? *Porra loca*! You know what I'm asking. I just saw you yesterday with two GT's, that's what."

Bill caught Beth's eyes. He'd asked her what had happened when she'd returned from the meeting, and she'd told him she couldn't say. She then asked him to keep it between the two of them.

"One was Tenerife, but the other wasn't from the station," Absinthe said, looking to Bill before turning back to Beth and asking, "So, what gives, *gata*?"

"Just another debrief," Beth said.

She wanted to blurt out everything, but Annabelle had let her know in no uncertain terms that doing so could have drastic consequences. Beth understood why, but she was dying to share the fact that she'd been right all along.

"When are they going to leave you alone?" Bill said. "Shit, it isn't like we all haven't made a mistake sometime. Just let it go and move on. You need to start working off your debt, and you can't do that sitting here on your ass."

She kept the smile on her face. She hadn't gone into detail about what happened in the system with him, and he either hadn't heard or didn't believe the theory that she was hiding a Class A planet. All he knew was that she'd destroyed the gate and owed the company big time for it.

For a brief moment, she was tempted to confide in the two, and she'd even opened her mouth to speak before common sense took over.

"Yes, you were about to say . . . ?" Absinthe prompted.

"I was about to say that they'll be done when they're done."

"That's not right. I think I'll hit up Martinez after chow," Bill said. "See what she can do to fix this."

"No, just let it be," Beth said, too quickly.

Absinthe gave her a sharp look.

Just relax, Beth. Take it easy.

She didn't want to get Martinez, or anyone else, for that matter, poking around the situation. Ignoring Absinthe's piercing glare, she swirled her last Vargas Finger in the remnants of the tolly sauce before popping it into her mouth, then licked the tips of her fingers.

"With that, I'm done," she said, standing. "I'm going to watch Episode Seven. Since your mission was cancelled, are you up for that?"

"Sure, let me finish my burger," he said, smashing what was left of it into his mouth.

"Episode Seven? Can I crash the party?" Absinthe asked. "My mission was canc'ed, too."

"You already watched the entire season," Beth said.

"I know, *gata*, but this episode is when Horti—"

"Stop!" Beth and Bill yelled in unison.

"You can come watch, but you've got to keep your mouth shut," Beth said.

"And I've got dibs on the bed. You get to sit on the floor," Bill added.

Beth waited on the other two, and in a few moments, the three were walking down the passage to her room.

Soon, my brother and sister, I can tell you what happened. Until then, just bear with me.

Chapter 5

Beth's PA softly chimed. She still had it in sleep mode despite being awake for the last hour—awake, but still in the rack. It wasn't as if her schedule was full.

She was going to ignore it, but sleep had left her for good, so she reached over to grab it.

Hell.

It was from accounting. Her monthly pay. By law, HB was only allowed to deduct 50% of her pay each month to tally against what she owed for the gate. The problem was that it was based on her average monthly pay for the last year. This month, what with the dry wells and not being sent out on a mission for the last three weeks, she'd earned less than the deduction. She was *down* 84.52 BC for the month.

She let her head fall back on her pillow, dropping her PA on the deck.

How am I going to tell Ina?

Her mother counted on whatever Beth could send her to help keep the extended family going. This month, that was going to be a big fat zero.

Whatever happiness Beth had felt after her meeting with Mzee Patel-Amand had long since evaporated like the morning mist. She'd become frustrated with the lack of missions. She no longer expected a bonus for SG-4021, but she wanted a chance to earn her living. Instead, she was being ignored. She was a ghost, simply existing.

She'd seen PA6 Martinez, asking her to find out when she'd be put back into the rotation, but nothing had come of that. Two days ago, she'd made an appointment with Mzee Teneriffe, but while she'd been sympathetic, she reminded Beth that she had no power to affect the way HB ran their business. If they didn't want her to go out on missions, that was their prerogative.

Beth left the meeting and steamed all the way back to her stateroom. Bill had chosen that moment to ask if she'd finally ordered Season Four of *The Justice Navy*, and she'd snapped, telling him she wasn't his mother and for him to get a life.

She felt bad when he'd recoiled, hurt evident on his face, but not bad enough to apologize. She knew he was just trying to cheer her up, but all she wanted was to be left alone. She did try to find him the next morning to mend things, but he'd already left on his next mission.

Beth stared at her overhead, lacking the initiative to get up and get dressed. Why bother? She sunk into a pool of self-pity. None of this was fair. It wasn't her fault that she'd been sent to that God-cursed system. It wasn't her fault that through some amazing flying, she wasn't killed and was able to get back to Nexus Prime and warn mankind.

Her PA chimed again from the deck where she dropped it. She wanted to ignore it, she *tried* to ignore it, but habits were ingrained. With a sigh, she rolled over onto her belly and picked it up. The voice call icon flashed at her, but without an identifier. She was tempted to cut the connection, but curiosity overcame her.

"Yeah, what is it?"

"I'd like you to meet me at G-08-106," a deep male voice said.

"Who is this?"

"I'll tell you when you arrive. Do not tell anyone you're coming."

The hell I'll come.

People just didn't wander off for clandestine meetings. Crime was low aboard stations, especially ones run by zaibatsus like HB. Still, there were the occasional assaults, rapes, and even murders. Beth didn't have any enemies that she knew of, but she was on the bad side of the company. She was pretty sure A8 Huhn was still pissed at her, but would he stoop to actually hurting her? She didn't think so, but was it worth taking a chance?

"Pilot Dalisay, are you there?"

"Uh . . . yes, I'm here."

"Are you coming?"

She wanted to say no. She knew she should say no. Let whoever it was come to her, or they could meet in the galley. But there was something about his voice that triggered something in her mind—and her curiosity was growing.

Her *ina* had always told her when she was a child that her curiosity would either make or break her. What was going on? The only way to find out would be to go.

"Yes, give me a few minutes, and I'll be on my way."

The man on the other side cut the connection while Beth jumped out of the rack. She looked at her reflection in her mirror. Her hair was tousled—snarled was more like it. She gave her underarms a sniff, then recoiled. If she'd gotten up at a normal hour, she would have already taken her sonicjet and been presentable. There was no getting around that now.

She ran her fingers through her short hair, yanking out the snarls. Running the water, she splashed her face first, her armpits second. She gave them another sniff—better, but not good. Pulling up her rack and exposing the storage compartment, she looked for her pit spray before remembering she'd run out the day before last and hadn't bought any more.

What to use, what to use . . .

A soft lilac dispenser caught her eye. Hesitantly, she picked it up. Her *ina* had given it to her after her last leave, telling her that "a woman must always feel fresh." Beth was a practical woman and didn't buy into marketing, but she didn't want to argue with her mother, so she'd just put the container in her bag.

"FemiNu" was printed on it in large pink letters, an image of a lily beneath the name. Beth tilted the dispenser at the air above her and gave it a tiny pump, leaning in to sniff.

It's not bad.

With a shrug, she aimed it at her armpits, giving each one a shot. She took another sniff, and while a little flowery, they were better than they'd been before.

"Thanks, *Ina*," she said.

She threw on a pair of station coveralls and gave one last look in the mirror. She was presentable—barely. Cupping her hand over her mouth, she breathed out.

Not good.

And of course, she was out of breath blasts.

I've really got to get stocked back up on the essentials, she thought as she looked around her stateroom.

She'd been letting her frustration impact the normal necessities of everyday life.

That's going to change, starting today.

The little lilac dispenser she'd dropped on her rack caught her eye again.

What the heck, why not?

She picked it up, pointed it at her mouth, and gave a full blast, almost gagging. She spit the stuff out, scraping her tongue against her top teeth. Lifting her hand, she checked her breath again, and to her surprise, it was actually better.

This was as good as she was going to get, so it was time to move. She stuck her head out the door, looking to see if anyone was around. The voice told her not to tell anyone, and she considered disobeying and doing just that. No one was around, though, so she slipped out and made her way to the carriage. Within moments, she was being whisked to the G Deck.

"This had better be good," she said quietly, anxiously waiting for the door to open.

Beth had never been to G Deck. As far as she knew, it was a maintenance deck, with shops and storage. Pilots would never have a reason to be there. She thought she might be conspicuous in her deep blue overalls of the Exploration Corps, but the one person who saw her in the passage never even gave her a second glance. Beth made her way to 08-106, which was a nondescript door without a sign.

That gave her pause. An unmarked space did not seem like a normal spot for a legitimate meeting. There wasn't even a chime button. She almost turned around, but she'd come this far, and she wanted to find out what was up. She wasn't stupid, though.

She'd passed an open storeroom back down the passage, so she retreated and looked inside. No one was there, but she did spot a shelf of assorted parts. A quick look revealed an angled metal bar that would do in a pinch, so she snatched it.

This will do, she thought as she hefted it a few times.

She returned to 08-106, and holding the bar behind her back, knocked. A moment later, the door opened.

Whoever Beth had thought would be waiting for her, this wasn't him. A jet-black GT stood holding the door open, so black that light seemed to be sucked into him like a black hole, never to escape.

"Are you coming in, or do you plan to hit me with that club you're holding?" he asked in a deep, gravely voice.

Beth's arm had sunk down to her side, the bar almost touching the deck.

"Sorry, Mzee," she said, keeping her eyes locked on his as she squatted and placed the bar to the side.

"Well, come in, Pilot Dalisay."

Beth entered what looked to be a small conference room, tastefully if not extravagantly furnished. She stepped forward, conscious of the looming presence now behind her, knowing he could crush her with one blow. Her knees trembled.

Most GTs liked to expose a lot of skin—all the better to show off. Those in official positions with the Directorate wore singlets in Directorate maroon, with their rank and department on their left thigh. Those at the highest ranks had gold trim around the cuffs, neckline, and arm seam. This GT was dressed in a casual transparent Windsor and grey slacks.

The GT might run humankind, but that didn't mean they all supported the directorate. They had criminals, just as the norms had. Even those skirting the law were not above straying past the lines if business demanded it. Beth had knowledge of something that could turn humankind on its head, and she was very aware that factions might not want that knowledge to get out before they developed a plan. Beth had promised silence, but she knew where she rated in the trillions of humans, and her elimination wouldn't even register a blip on the scale of humanity.

She wished she still had the bar in her hand.

She walked over to the small conference table, first heading to the left side, and at the last moment, changing direction to go to the right. She slowly turned to face the GT once more.

He might have cracked the tiniest of smiles, but as dark as he was, she couldn't be sure. It was difficult to focus on the man.

"Please, sit," he said, pointing at one of the chairs.

Beth warily pulled the chair out and sat. Of course, it was built for normal-sized people, so she had to sit on the edge of the chair, arms on the table. The GT pulled back a GT-sized chair and sat comfortably.

Beth took note of that. There were five such chairs in the room: two at the table, three back against the far bulkhead. GTs used this space on a regular basis, then. Why such a nondescript room, she didn't have a clue, only that they probably didn't want any meetings to become common knowledge.

"Pilot Dalisay, thank you for coming to meet me. I am Commander Grey Tuominen, Navy of the Humankind," he said, using the formal term for the Directorate Navy.

He must have seen her look of confusion, because he smiled, and said, "I'm in civvies now so as not to draw attention to my presence here at HB Station."

"Why hide that fact?" she blurted out before thinking.

If he took offense, he didn't show it, but answered, "I'm only here for a short time, and I didn't want to go through the red tape."

"But you're the Directorate Navy. You can go anywhere."

He smiled again, but not as broadly. "If necessary, yes, we can. However, for routine missions, we must ask permission to enter any space controlled by a zaibatsu."

That didn't make much sense to her. The Directorate Navy was the most powerful military force known to man. It was what gave the Directorate its power. Every zaibatsu contributed funds to keep it running. But that was a question for another time. What she wanted to know was why she'd been called to meet this commander.

"What can I do for you, sir? Are you here for my version of what happened?"

"No, not really, Pilot Dalisay. I've already reviewed your reports, and I've gone over the recorded data. I've seen enough of them." He paused a moment, then said, "Well, maybe one thing. Why did you take control of your Hummingbird while slinging around the gas giant?"

"Well, Mzee—"

"Commander."

"Uh . . . yes, Commander. I was being pursued by a hostile alien force. It had fired some sort of torpedoes at me, and they would reach me before I could get behind the planet. I tried to adjust my course to cut closer to the planet to shave off some time, but my AI wouldn't let me. Too dangerous, it said."

"So, you took over, flew a course that took your Hummingbird to the outer reaches of the exosphere, and skipped your craft around the planet."

"Yes, Mz . . . yes, Commander."

"And you thought you had the skill to do it?"

"Yes, Commander."

"Why?"

"With all due respect, Commander, why doesn't matter much now. I'm here today, so I was proven right."

The smile came back, and he nodded his acceptance of her logic. "You're correct, of course. You're here today, and on a professional level, I have to salute what was some exceptional piloting."

Beth felt the warm glow of pride. She didn't know this commander from Adam, but she welcomed the praise.

"And that brings us to why I made the trip from Sahra. Are you happy with your contract with HB?"

"Pardon me?"

"Simple question, Pilot. Are you happy with your situation here with the Hamdani Brothers?"

"The Hamdani Brothers are well-noted as one of the best corporations for pilots, particularly OPWs."

"You didn't answer the question, Pilot. Am I wasting my time here?"

I don't know why you are here, so how can I know if you are wasting your time?

He waited for her answer. Beth didn't know what she should say. It wasn't a good idea to badmouth the company that paid her paycheck, even if they were taking out more than what she earned.

The thought of that, the thought of having to tell her *ina* that there would be nothing coming this month, reignited her anger, and before she could govern herself, she blurted out, "No, I'm not."

"May I ask why?"

"Why? Because I am being punished. I *owe* them eighty-four BC for this month, for God's sake. They want me to pay for the gate that I destroyed following your regulations, that's why," she said. "And no one from the Directorate will intervene."

"We can't intervene, Pilot. We don't have the authority for this type of case." he said, watching her. "But is that the only reason you're not happy?"

"Do I need more?" When his expression didn't waver, she added, "Well, maybe there is."

"And what is that?"

She tried to marshal her thoughts. It suddenly hit her why she was so frustrated, and it was not only the money. It took her a moment to frame her words.

"I'm a pilot, Commander. But they won't let me fly. I'm sitting in my rack while the black calls me. I want—no, I need to fly."

She looked down at her fingernails, embarrassed. Being an Exploration Corps pilot was a job, nothing more, but it had grown on her. Deep space was singing its siren song, calling her, and she couldn't answer. If that wasn't a sign of weakness, she didn't know what was.

To her surprise, she looked back up to see what she perceived to be a look of satisfaction on the commander's face before he said, "How would you like to fly again, Pilot?"

"I would love to, Commander, but I don't think HB is going to schedule me again."

"I think I can change that, if you're interested."

Yeah, I'm interested, not that it makes any difference.

"You can't interfere with an unjust fine, so I don't think you can just tell the dispatcher to give me missions."

"True, I can't. As an officer of the Navy of Mankind, I hold exactly zero sway here. But if you were no longer part of HB, and you were in, say the Navy, I would have."

Beth's heart jumped for a second, hopeful, but then she laughed bitterly and said, "I'm still under contract."

OPW contracts were ironclad, except for the hiring company. There was no way she could break that contract.

"I have reason to believe that we can approach HB and buy out your contract."

"You *do* know I have a fine over my head? Over half-a-million."

He flicked his hand as if brushing away a fly.

"And then what, Commander?"

"And then? I think it would be obvious. I want you to join the Navy. I want you in my squadron."

"What? Me? I'm flattered, but I'm just a Hummingbird pilot, an OPW, I need to remind you. You get more volunteers than you can take, from what I've read."

"Yes, you are a Hummingbird pilot, one who was able to take it beyond its capabilities and escape an alien man-of-war. Not many would have both the balls and the skill to pull that off, and I want that kind of pilot in my squadron.

"I should give you a little more information. We have long suspected that there are Others out there. Odd readings here and there, things that didn't make sense by any other explanation. For the last three years, I've been in charge of developing a course of action should we ever meet them. Thanks to you, we have, and I am now standing up a new squadron. Our focus will be on the alien threat. Until we know just what we are facing, we cannot deploy the capital ships. Someone has to feel out the enemy, if they even *are* the enemy."

Beth started to protest, but he held up a hand to silence her. "Yes, one of their ships attacked you, but that might have been a knee-jerk reaction. We have to know for sure."

Beth bit back a retort, but he was right. If that was a mistake, and the aliens were friendly, then humanity didn't want to stumble into a war.

"I still don't know why me, Commander. There are a million pilots plying the black."

"Well, Mzee Teneriffe did ask if there was anything that could be done for you. I didn't pay that much heed until I saw how you handled your Hummingbird. Then I realized that out of all humanity, you are the only person who's faced these aliens, at least as far as we know. You are certainly the only human who has faced them and lived to tell the tale. I think that eminently qualifies you."

Beth began to feel the slight stirrings of hope. To get into the Navy? No one from her social ring could hope to achieve that.

"How would this work?"

"To get you into the Navy? I'll tell Mzee Teneriffe as soon as you accept, and she'll start the process. In a day or two, you'll leave Nexus Prime for Fleet Ops on Refuge. Eight weeks of boot camp—I can't pull enough strings to get you out of that—and you report to me. You're already a qualified pilot, so we can transfer that rating to the Navy, and you'll get snapped into your new ride at Type School."

Her ears perked up at that. He already mentioned capital ships, and if this was some sort of special squadron, they were probably flying skiffs or patrol craft. Most of her piloting skills should transfer, even if it would be like taking a flitter driver and giving them a bus. Her Hummingbird might not be the most powerful craft in the galaxy, but she'd showed it could take some aggressive flying. If she had to shift to the space-going version of a bus, at least she'd be out of debt and still in space.

"What would I be flying?"

"I didn't tell you that?" he asked, innocently.

Oh, hell, is it worse than a skiff?

"No, Commander, you didn't."

"Oh, in that case, we're flying Wasps. FX6 Kilos."

"Wasps!" she almost shouted.

"Why, yes. Is that a problem, Pilot Dalisay?" he said, the crooks of his obsidian mouth tilting up.

"I'm in, Commander. Oh, am I ever in!"

PART 2

Chapter 6

Naval Space Pilot Third Class Floribeth Salinas O'Shea Dalisay, Navy of Humankind, stepped around the Wasp, dutifully going through the checklist on her pad. Senior Chief Wolfwitz dogged her steps, looking over her shoulder. All the readouts for FT6-142 read green, but it was tradition, going back centuries, that pilots physically check their ships before taking off.

She tugged on the microshield array, then checked it off, wishing she could skip the rest of the steps and just take this beauty out into space. It took a force of will to methodically check off each step of the inspection.

It was hard to believe that she'd soon be flying an actual Wasp, the ultimate sports vehicle. This may be the "T," or training version, its weapons only dummies and without the still-classified capabilities of the "X" version she would be flying in the squadron, but it was still a Wasp. Fifteen weeks ago, she'd been a grounded Hummingbird pilot, and now she was at the pinnacle of single-seat flying.

Three days after meeting with Commander Tuominen at Nexus Prime, Beth was saying goodbye to Bill, Absinthe, and the rest, and leaving the HB station—not before Accountant Eight Huhn had tracked her down and told her she was still liable for her fine until Mzee Tenerife, who was also at her farewell party, told him to go pound sand. A few days later, she, along with close to 200 other recruits, was being sworn in to the Navy at the Naval Training Station, Region 1.

The next eight weeks sucked, to be blunt. By far the shortest and one of the oldest people in the company, she'd endured her share of harassment from her fellow recruits. "Sandblower," "Grandma," and "Housekeeper," were among the least insulting terms. All the time, she was aching to put some of the others in their place by telling them that while almost all her fellow recruits were going to be Seamen Apprentices doing scutwork in their various fields, she was not only going to be a petty officer, but a Wasp pilot.

Only she couldn't. The chief who had met her as she got off the ship had told her in no uncertain terms that she had to keep quiet. What the commander and his bosses were doing was highly unusual, and the fewer people who knew about it, the better. Beth got the impression that much of what VFX-99 was doing was unusual, not just what was happening with her.

So, she put up with the hazing, she put up with the runs where her short legs were a handicap—why did sailors, except for the commando-types, have to run, she wondered while laboring through each exhausting run—she put up with the insults by keeping her eye on the prize.

And here was the prize. After logging in her 18 flights in the simulator, she was going out for the real thing. She ran her hand over the smooth bow of the Wasp, unable to resist. With only two more items on her checklist, she should be underway in mere moments.

Second-to-last was to check the vector ports. Unlike her little Hummingbird, a Wasp had the same FC powerplant as capital ships. What made a Wasp unique was the vectoring system that could channel the thrust from various ports, making it extremely maneuverable. Larger ships had bow thrusters which assisted maneuverability under the same concept, but within the Navy, at least, no other vessel could vector the thrust in almost any direction.

A Wasp had 12 vector ports in addition to the main array. Beth checked the readout first. All 12 were closed, the system green. Next was a visual and physical check. She gave each of the lower ones a quick glance, then ran her fingers over the port, seeking any misalignment. She hurried, anxious to get into space. Too short to reach the upper ones, she pulled her little stepladder up so she could climb and reach the ports. She gave the Port 7, the upper midships port, a quick look. Like the first six, it looked fine. She ran her fingers over it, already looking to its twin, a meter to the starboard, and almost checked it off when something registered with her.

Did I just feel something?

She straightened up on her ladder for a moment while she contemplated what she'd just felt, then leaned forward and gave it a careful look again. It still looked good. She ran her fingers once more over the seam.

There it is.

Very faint, almost imperceptible, she had felt something. She glanced up at the chief, who looked bored.

She checked the readout again, specifically pulling up Port 7 in isolation. Green. She hit the reset, and within seconds, the light turned green again.

What now?

She reached out one more time, rubbing her finger over the featureless skin of the Wasp, and now she was sure she felt the tiniest imperfection.

"Are you going to dawdle here all day, Dalisay? I've got things to do, even if you don't," Chief Wolfwitz said, his voice expressing his displeasure.

Behind him, NA2 Rymer, whose sole purpose in life was to keep FT6-142 spaceworthy, looked concerned.

Beth still couldn't see any imperfection in the seam. It looked fine, and the readouts were green. Still, she had felt something.

A Wasp pushing the performance envelope underwent tremendous forces, forces that wanted to tear the fighter apart. A minor technical mishap at .91C could have catastrophic results.

But I'm not going .91C today, and I really want to try this baby out.

"Well, Dalisay? Are you going to fly today, or are you chickening out?"

She bristled at the insult and was ready to check the last ports and finish the inspection. She wasn't hesitating because she was afraid. The Wasp checked out green, and so she trusted it.

Ah, hell. I can't do it. Regulations are regulations.

"I'm sorry, Chief. I can't up-check this fighter," she said, her heart falling.

By giving it an official down-check, she was taking the Wasp offline for several hours at a minimum. It would take Rymer's time, Senior Chief Win's time, then Lieutenant Franks' time as safety officer to up-check the craft again.

And she would miss her flight until she could be slotted in again.

"Why not, Petty Officer Dalisay?" he asked.

"I felt an imperfection around Port Seven."

The chief took her readout, looked at it, and said, "It reads here as green."

"I know that, Chief. But I also know what I felt."

"And you, a boot, know more than the readouts, more than Rymer here?"

"I'm not saying I do," Beth said, feeling miserable. "All I know is that I feel something that shouldn't be there. I can't up-check this craft."

"And that's your final word?" the chief asked, hands on his hips as he leaned into her, his eyes ten centimeters from hers.

"Yes, Chief. That's my final word," she said, not willing to back down.

"Very well," he said, his tone completely changed from antagonistic to . . . well, normal. He looked to NA2 Rymer and said, "Take her back and bring out 131."

Rymer winked, a smile on his face, and said, "I've already got her ready, baby seat installed."

What? Was that a test?

Beth was shorter than any other pilot, too short for the standard Wasp seat. For her to fly, she needed an additional insert installed, nicknamed a "baby seat." She wasn't the only pilot who needed one, and they took only a few minutes to connect, but Rymer wouldn't have already had it in 131 unless he expected her to fly that instead of 142.

"Since you didn't want 142, you've got 131 and another inspection to make," he said.

"I thought you said you had things to do, Chief," she said.

"Don't worry about that, Dalisay. I've got all the time in the world."

****

Fifty minutes later, Beth was sitting in FT6-131, ready for launch. Her heart was racing. This was nothing like waiting for a Hummingbird launch, which was done entirely under the scout's power. The Wasp had FC engines, and the thrust particles could wear down a hangar in short order. She'd seen ancient videos of old airplanes taking off of wet-water carriers, shot off of a steam catapult, and that was as close as she could imagine what was going to happen next. Her Wasp was about to be slung out into space at 40 Gs, well within the fighter's ability to compensate and keep her body whole, but still, quicker than she'd ever had hit her at once before.

She didn't want to think of what would happen to her if the compensators failed and was suddenly glad that she'd done the physical inspection, green display lights or not.

"FT6-131, are you green for launch?" the cat officer asked over the net.

"Roger, green, CAT."

"Understand green. Standby, launch in five . . . four . .
."

Beth tensed up, despite the fact that if something did go wrong, her tensing up wouldn't make the slightest bit of difference.

". . . three . . . two . . . one . . . launch."

And Beth was out of the station, just like that, hurtling through space along the launch path. Within seconds, the ship routed the angry beast of her powerplant, and photons poured through cerroalloy tubes, pushing her at a mind-numbing acceleration. The compensators were up to the task, and combined with her flight suit, she felt fine. Some pilots hated the feel of the constant battle between compensators and physics, but not Beth. The sensations never bothered her.

She kept on the assigned trajectory, the Wasp still under the space traffic coordinator's control. She could take over in an emergency, but until she was in her assigned training area, she was little more than a passenger.

Oh, hell, no I'm not!

She might not be controlling her fighter, but she had to go through her next checklist—she had so many of them that she was surprised the Navy didn't have a checklist for taking a dump. It took her less than a minute, and everything was up and ready.

Her display didn't look much different from the one on her old Hummingbird. She was hurtling through space, just like before. As soon as she reached her training area, though, things would be different as she put her Wasp through its paces.

Her excitement level rose the closer she got, and she almost yelled out when the STC told her, "You are now released. Stay within your TA, and happy flying!"

Beth immediately took control of the Wasp and pushed it over into a wide, sweeping arc. As her speed built up, the arc flattened out, and she approached the boundary of her free flight zone.

"Time for the vectors."

She shunted power to Ports 1 and 2, swinging the nose of the fighter to the right, pushing the little fighter to its limit. She felt a slight shift in her body as the compensators tried to keep her from becoming a red mush at the bottom of her cockpit. She watched her track on the display, and to her amazement, she could see her course tighten into an almost unbelievably tight arc.

"I've got to see this for real," she said, pulling up visuals.

Contrary to holovids, fighters did not go into dogfights by peering through ancient canopies. Speeds were so fast and distances were so long that the human eye was not good enough. Eyes could be used for docking and other low-speed, close-up evolutions, but not much else. Every pilot, however, liked to bring up the visuals and just absorb the sights, especially closer to the galactic core.

Refuge was closer to the galactic rim, but stargazing wasn't why Beth shifted to visuals. She pulled the Wasp into another turn, this time vectoring thrust to Ports 3 and 4. In her Hummingbird, turns were slow and ponderous, and on visuals, she could barely see the stars shift as she came about. With the Wasp, the stars were moving like the night sky on speed. She could see how fast her fighter was turning.

And this wasn't even close to the limit. FT6-131 was a trainer, and the Navy wanted their new pilots back in one piece. As with all trainers, the 131 was "de-tuned." This was the baby version of what Beth would be flying later.

One hell of a baby, though.

For the next hour, Beth put the Wasp through its paces. On her next training run, she'd be following a mission plan, eventually working up to offensive operations. But for now, the Navy was willing to let her just have fun.

Beth pulled a 180, a procedure to reverse course that pushed almost half of her thrust out of Ports 11 and 12. It was sloppy, and she'd be able to do much better with a mission-ready Wasp and a G-shot, but she was still impressed with the results.

"Oh, good girl," she said, patting the fighter's display.

She was about to try again when the dreaded call came in. "FT6-131, playtime's over for today. Head to Sierra-Charlie-Whiskey 03482125, 7678935, 2356921 where we'll take over and bring you home."

With a heavy heart, she punched in the coordinates on the display, and keeping manual control, flew the Wasp to the turnover. She settled into her seat as the STC took over.

She was flying high, however. The trainer had been great, but it only hinted at what a real Wasp could do.

"It *is* a real Wasp," she reminded herself.

As soon as she whispered the words, it hit her.

She was now a Wasp pilot

Chapter 7

"You ready to get to work, Petty Officer Dalisay?" Commander Tuominen asked, stepping from around his desk. "And at ease, for God's sake."

"Yes, sir, I'm ready," she said, relaxing her position of attention.

"Good to hear it. We've got an exercise in three days, and I want you to be part of it."

"Uh, sir, I don't have a ship yet. I just came over from Type School."

"Then what are you doing here gabbing with me?"

"Uh . . . they told us at boot—"

"Hell, Dalisay, calm down. I'm not serious."

Beth wondered if the commander knew just how imposing he looked. She'd actually been worried she'd done something wrong.

"You do have to get going, and I'm snowed under with paperwork, but if I can't take a moment to welcome my newest pilot, well, something's wrong. Take a seat."

He slid into an oversized chair that fit his frame while Beth hopped up onto one next to him. It wasn't quite as bad as the one in the conference room where they'd first met, but she wished there was something a little smaller, at least so she could rest her feet on the deck.

"I've been watching your progress, and you did well in Type School, scoring in the 95th percentile."

Beth didn't even know they were being ranked, but she should have. If she thought HB was detail-oriented before, she now knew the Navy was far, far worse (or better, depending on the frame of reference).

"Chief Garcia's got your ship primed and ready, and I want to you to get at least ten hours in before the exercise. The X models are a lot different than the T's at Type School."

"I did a check-flight in a Bravo, sir," Beth offered.

The commander gave a short chuckle, then said, "Not even close.

"Anyway, are you locked into berthing?"

"No, sir. I just got here from Charlie."

Charlie Station was the largest of the stations around Refuge, housing over 2,000 smaller craft and with gates for 20 capital ships at a time. The administrative headquarters, as well as boot camp, family housing, the naval hospital, and scores of other facilities were on the planet's surface, but most of the force was in orbit or scattered throughout the system. VFX-99 was located on Sierra Station, which was carved out of a rogue moon that had long ago broken free from the system's main gas giant. Sierra was a secure station with limited access. As far as Beth knew, VFX-99 and a SEAL team were the only units stationed there.

"Well, we're a little tight on space here, so you'll be doubling up with Petty Officer Hamlin. Sorry about that."

"No problem, sir," she said.

She'd just spent eight weeks in a squadbay with 200 of her not-so-closest friends, then shared a six-person space with other petty officers at Type School.

"OK, well, I want you to get your final fitting and synch with your Wasp today, so when you leave here, go to the hangar and get that done. Then worry about your berthing. Did Master Chief brief you on that situation?"

"Master Chief Orinoco wasn't in his office, sir, so I just came here."

"I'm sure she'll be back soon, and you really need to see her. No, I'll let her know you'll stop by later. You go get synched," he said, ignoring that Beth had assumed the master chief to be male. "In fact," he continued, taking a look at his wristcomp, "I'm going to cut this short. We'll have a longer chat later, but I really want you to get synched.

"Chief Garcia, are you ready for Petty Officer Dalisay?" he spoke into his comp.

"Primed and ready, sir."

"OK, I'm sending her down now. Let me know if there's any holdup." He looked up at Beth and said, "Chief's in Bay 3. It's a little convoluted here, so ask your comp. And with that, I'll let you go."

He stood up and held out a hand, dwarfing Beth's as he shook it.

"What about my gear, sir?"

"Where is it?"

"Right outside your hatch, sir. I didn't know what to do with it."

The commander strode over to the hatch, reached out, and easily dragged in the seabag that Beth had struggled with.

"It'll be fine here. Now go."

"Aye-aye, sir," Beth said, coming to attention before performing a credible about-face and marching out of the office. She whispered "Bay 3" into the comp, and the route to where her own Wasp waited illuminated on her ocular implant.

The wrist comps were pretty righteous pieces of gear, each one probably costing a scout pilots annual salary. She didn't even know half of what it could do, but what she had discovered so far was pretty impressive. Just take the simple route to Bay 3. The comp had interacted with the insubstantial implant in her right eye, and she could see the route laid out for her, as if it was painted on the deck.

"Switch route to pink," she said, and immediately the route glowed a shocking pink. "Rainbow." The wristcomp complied.

She giggled as she followed the path, then guiltily looked around. She was supposed to be a professional fighter pilot, not a little girl with a new toy. No one was in the passage, so she put on a serious face and followed the winding rock corridors as her comp led her.

Being inside a planetoid was a little disconcerting. New Cebu was an empty, open planet without any of the lush foliage of the Philippine Islands, the home country of the planet's first settlers, but a person could see for miles in any direction. Bally's World, at least around the resort at which she was a housekeeper, was sculpted to please the masses, and Refuge had wide open spaces as well. HB's station at Nexus Prime and the Navy's Charlie Station were confined, but with nice, manufactured walls. This was different. She reached out to touch the walls, running her fingers along the rough surface. It seemed as if all the O2 inside could just eventually seep out.

They say it's safer in an underground station than one in orbit, she told herself.

It was probably true, but it didn't feel that way.

She passed several people, a lean man in a black workout singlet stopping to stare unabashedly at her as she passed. She was tempted to tell him to go shower—he reeked as she passed—but she held her tongue. In a real station, the air circulation would have whisked his smell away.

She arrived at the hatch into Bay 3. Tentatively, she leaned into the scanner, wondering if she was in the system yet. She needn't have worried—the door opened into a large— no, *huge*—bay. At least 30 Wasps were out on the deck, a dozen or so being worked on by sailors in green overalls.

Beth was lost. She had no idea to whom she was supposed to go. At the far end of the bay, she spotted two figures in tan overalls standing over a Wasp. Tan signified chiefs, and as she didn't see any others, she made her way through the parked craft to them. Several sailors stopped to stare as she walked by in her pilot blues, her gold pilot's wings conspicuous on her chest. She subconsciously tried to walk taller before she realized what she was doing and forced herself to relax. They'd just have to get used to her.

She knew she was already an oddity in the squadron without even considering her height. The Navy's pilots were split about 60/40 officer-to-enlisted, and most of the enlisted were aboard the bigger capital ships, where officers commanded the bridge. Most of the remainder of the enlisted pilots handled shuttles and ships' launches. It wasn't until six or seven years prior that the Navy, in what some called another social experiment, started bringing in the best and the brightest of the enlisted pilots into single-seat fighters and scouts. Beth had already checked the squadron's mix. Out of 54 pilots, three were warrants, and a grand total of 13 were enlisted. As a new PO3, Beth was the junior-most. Probably half of all the enlisted sailors in the squadron outranked her, but she would still have the absolute and final say about her Wasp.

"You must be our new pilot," the first chief said as Beth walked up.

"Yes, Master Chief. Petty Officer Dalisay."

Master Chief Orinoco was a good foot or more taller than Beth, but she had a much larger presence even taking into account her height. Her voice was asbestos-hard, almost grating on her ears.

"Well, the skipper wants you ready for the next exercise, so I'll leave you with Senior Chief here to get you synched. If it isn't too much trouble, I'd like to talk to you when you're done here."

The Command Master Chief's words were pleasant, but the tone was not, and Beth's inner warning kicked off a few alarm signals.

What did I do?

The Master Chief strode off, and Senior Chief Garcia called out, "Frye! Your pilot's here. Get Tasha to bring over her helmet so we can get this done before chow."

Beth turned around, eager to see her helmet interface. If her wristcomp cost a year's worth of her previous salary, the helmet had to cost more like five years' worth. This put the *high* into high-tech. Her head had been scanned to a micron, and that data was sent to one of the two manufacturers of the helmets in the entire galaxy. This would be the first time she would see it.

As they waited, she was going to ask the senior chief if she'd said something wrong to the master chief, but she decided to keep quiet. She could just be reading into things that didn't exist. After a minute, a tall, gangly, and very young spaceman came running up, carrying a case, followed by a heavy-set woman in KenCorp overalls. The spaceman set the case on the workbench, and the civilian tech opened it and then casually removed the helmet inside. It looked small in her hands, but the value was in what was it could do. Beth gingerly took it from the tech. It was surprisingly light, much lighter than the generic helmets she'd used at Type School.

"Well, put it on," the civilian said.

"Oh, sorry."

She slipped it on, and it felt as if it had a mind of its own, like a puppy snuggling in on a cold night. She could barely feel it on her head, the interface was so smooth.

"Give me the torch, Frye," the tech told the young spaceman.

When Beth had taken it, the faceshield had looked black, but looking through it, it was as if there was nothing between her eyes and the bay. She knew the visor was a thick, opaque ceramic, but the image shown against the inside was faultless. She instinctively reached up to touch her face, and her finger stopped fast after hitting the visor.

"Pretty real, huh?" the senior chief asked.

"Amazing."

At Type School, Beth had worn a generic helmet, relying on her ocular implant for displays. Still, that had been far better than the clunky helmet displays they'd had with HB (which was why most Hummingbird pilots didn't even wear them, relying on the scout's heads-up display instead), but this was a leap up and beyond, and it wasn't even synched yet.

"I'm going to start the helmet synch," the tech told her. "Raise your hand the moment you hear something."

Beth could hear the hustle and bustle of a busy hangar, and she was about to raise her hand when the sound cut off. The tech entered some data or instructions into the instrument she was holding—Beth assumed it was the "torch" she'd asked for. A soft, high-pitched beep sounded in her right ear, and Beth raised her hand. The tech studied her torch for a moment, and the sound stopped.

"You can put your hand down now."

Her fingers tapped and swiped on the torch, then the same sound started in her left ear. That wasn't quite accurate. Beth knew that she wasn't actually hearing through her ears. She'd had microfibers threaded under her scalp before reporting to Type School, the transmitters boring into her skull at key points. The "sound" was bypassing her ears and directly stimulating her cerebrum's temporal lobes. From her perspective, though, it was normal hearing.

The tech fiddled with her torch another minute, told her not to blink, then pointed it at her, a bright light blinding her.

Ah, that's why it's called a torch.

The tech kept it shining for 20 seconds or so before switching it off.

She checked the readout for a few seconds, then said, "OK, you're good to go."

"That's it?" Beth asked, surprised.

"That's it for the helmet. We've still got to synch it with your fighter," she said, tilting her head at the ship.

"Oh. It's just that I thought it would take longer. My fitting at Type School took an hour."

This helmet was supposed to be more capable, so to go through the process in a few minutes surprised her.

The tech laughed, then said, "That's why it was so quick here. I already had your brain dump. Knew where we had to start. And this little baby," she said, patting her torch, "is top-of-the-line.

"Now *that*," she said, pointing to the fighter, "is going to take you quite a bit longer.

"I'll let Jorge know I'm done and send him over," she told the senior chief.

"Thanks, Tasha. You're the best."

"Damned right I am!"

"Should I get into my fighter?" Beth asked as the tech walked away.

The senior chief shrugged, then said, "We can't start synching you until Jorge gets here, but why the hell not? I imagine you're anxious to check out your baby. Frye, power up the systems."

"Yes, Senior Chief," the spaceman said, and a moment later, the lights inside the console lit up.

"Well?" the senior chief asked Beth.

She didn't need him to say anything else. She didn't have a stepladder yet, but there were foot indents that would disappear back into the hull once the fighter was underway. It was a reach, but she got her foot into the bottom indent, then using the leg still planted on the deck of the hangar, hopped up, grasping the edge of the cockpit. After that, it was easy to scramble up and slide into the fighter's seat.

Ultra-cool, she thought, excitement threatening to make her head explode. *And it's mine!*

"How does she feel?" the senior chief asked.

"Not bad," she said, as nonchalantly as she could.

It felt far better than "not bad." This is what she was born to do, and by God's miracle, she, a little girl from the barangays had somehow been plucked from obscurity to be given a freaking Wasp. She couldn't believe how lucky she was. She slid her right hand into the control sleeve and tapped out the command to engage thrust—she knew, of course, that the powerplant was not lit, but she imagined the Wasp streaking across the black.

"She'll feel better as we get you synched in. Give us an hour, and you'll feel like she's a part of you."

Except that it took almost three hours. Jorge, another KenCorp civilian tech, was methodical, and he wasn't pleased with her seat. It had been printed based on Beth's body specs, but even after some adjustments, both by printing a seat insert and pounding it with a wrench, he declared it a total wash. He ordered an entire new seat be printed, which took over 40 minutes.

Beth was excited to have her own Wasp, but she was getting bored, standing around doing nothing, then becoming little more than a mannikin being dressed by a designer. Finally, Jorge was satisfied, and the lieutenant called over for his check and sign-off.

"Frye, power her down, then get to chow. You, too, Dalisay. I'll find out when you're scheduled for your shakedown, and let you know."

"I've still got my gear in the CO's office, Senior Chief. Should I take care of my berthing first?"

"Hell, Dalisay. You're a damned petty officer, a pilot to boot. I'm not going to lead you by the hand around here. Do what you want—just be here tomorrow when I tell you."

Even if she was a petty officer, she'd been a recruit, then a student, and in both cases, she'd been following a set schedule, with someone else telling her what to do and when to do it. She had to get it in her mind that she was expected to be much more self-reliant.

"Roger, that, Senior Chief. I'll handle it."

She gave Spaceman Frye her helmet, the rumbling in her stomach making the decision that it was chow first, berthing second. She started to walk off but turned back for one last look at the fighter. She gave it one last possessive pat on the bow.

It wasn't just any Wasp. It was *her* Wasp.

Chapter 8

Beth leaned against the passageway bulkhead, eyes closed. That had not gone well.

She'd never made it to chow. She'd remembered that the command master chief had told her to check in after the synch, so she'd stopped by her office, expecting to leave a message, but the master chief was there and called her in. For a good hour, Beth had sat quietly in the chair across from the squadron's senior enlisted sailor, a member of the squadron's "Big Three" of commander, XO, and command master chief.

Most of the time had been spent with the master chief telling Beth about herself and her philosophy on life. The master chief was a glass-half-empty type of person who seemed to believe that sailors did best when their feet were held to the fire. Beth knew the type—people suspicious about the motives of others—and she didn't exactly mesh well with them.

At first, Beth just sat there, nodding, as the master chief when on. She had authority over Beth, true, but as a pilot, Beth thought she'd be somewhat protected from her control. At least, that was how PO1 Muhamed, back at Type School, had explained the dynamics of the new enlisted pilots.

Listening to the master chief, though, Beth wasn't sure that would be the case.

After giving Beth her history, she made it clear that she owned Beth. Sure, as a pilot, Beth would be working directly for her flight commander, Lieutenant Hadley. However, "to be

100% clear," when she was not actually flying, Beth belonged to her.

Through other comments, it also became 100% clear that the master chief did not approve of enlisted pilots, and even more disapproved of Beth's unorthodox jump from spaceman recruit to petty officer third class. Comments such as "Don't think you're going to sit on your ass and escape normal duties," and, "I'm putting you on the watch list starting the day after the next exercise's endex," pretty much made the woman's point.

Beth thought the master chief would keep going, but a call came in that required her attention, so with an "I'm watching you, Dalisay," she let Beth go. Too late for chow, though. The station was small enough that it didn't have 24-hour service, and Beth would have to wait until midrats to calm her angry belly.

She took ten deep breaths, calming herself. She'd been up against far more in her life, and she wasn't going to let an asshole, even one with power over her, affect her. Pasting a smile on her face, she went next door to the CO's office to retrieve her seabag, entered the space designator that the master chief had given her into her wristcomp, then dragged her seabag, following the path to her quarters. She started to buzz the entry button, in case her new bunkmate was inside, but thought *screw it* and waved her wrist comp over the access, opening the hatch.

The space was a little bigger than her quarters at HB: about ten feet deep and five feet wide. There was a fold-out desk at the far bulkhead and two bunks along the right-hand side. What caught her attention, though, was the woman in mismatched underwear lying on the bottom rack and watching something on a screen that folded down from underneath the top bunk.

"Well, Satan's nuts, girl, you're a fucking hobbit!" the woman said, folding up her screen and swinging her legs around to sit up at the edge of her bunk.

Beth stared at the woman—her new bunkmate—and a spark of anger began to blossom within her. She'd just put up with a ration of shit from the master chief, and she sure as hell wasn't going to put up with any more from this . . . this shaved-headed freak.

PO2 Hamlin had impossibly bright red hair—on half of her head. The other half was shaved, leaving a tiny bit of stubble in geometric patterns. She had three huge rings piercing her right nostril and one running through both her upper and lower lip on the right side of her mouth. Beth wondered for a moment if she'd stumbled into the wrong quarters and the woman was a civilian tech, not a naval petty officer.

"Don't stand out there gawking, girl; get your ass in here and let me look at you."

She jumped out of the rack, and Beth saw her new roomie was almost as short as she was. The woman pulled Beth by the arm into the space, and the hatch closed behind them.

"Hell, turn around," she said, physically turning Beth away.

Beth was about to protest when she felt her bunkmate's butt up against hers, then her hand pressing down on the top of her head.

"I fucking knew it. I've got at least four centimeters on you. I'm no longer the squadron sandblower," she said, turning a bewildered Beth back around.

"How tall are you?"

"Uh, four-foot . . . uh, a hundred-and-thirty-seven centimeters."

"And I'm one-forty-one. Boom!" she shouted, slapping the top bunk. "Mercy Hamlin, your bunkmate. But you can call me 'No Mercy,' 'cause I don't give none."

That's not going to happen.

"So, welcome to the Stingers, Floribeth. Do I call you that? Anyway, welcome. We've been waiting for you, and you've got to spill. So, what were they like?"

The rapid-fire comments, none seemingly connected, confused Beth. "Beth. Most people call me Beth. And what were who like?"

Mercy rolled her eyes, then said, "The fucking aliens, of course."

Beth could feel her face going white. That was supposed to be a closely-held secret.

"You know?"

Mercy laughed, filling the small stateroom with light. "Of course, I know. We all know. Even the snake eaters here on Sierra. Why do you think we even exist?"

"I don't know. I thought—"

"We've seen the recordings, but how did it feel? Satan's nuts, girl. What was going on in that little gourd of yours?"

Beth's defenses were up, but the almost overwhelming enthusiasm of Mercy was breaking them down.

"I was just trying to survive," she said, leaving it at that.

"You did a little more than that, sister."

"No, really. I was scared, and I was running."

Mercy snorted, then said, "Yeah, and in a piece of shit corporate scout. You've got big balls, girl."

Beth felt a surge of defensiveness. Her Hummingbird was not that bad of a craft.

Well, compared to a Wasp, maybe it was.

"Believe me. I'm not brave."

Mercy snorted again and said, "Then you're in the wrong place now. But the Commander, he don't make no mistakes like this. You belong here."

"The command master chief sure doesn't think so," Beth said before she could stop herself.

"Or No Go? She doesn't think anyone's good enough, especially none of us peon enlisted swine."

"That doesn't make any sense. She's enlisted, too."

"But she ain't no pilot, and she don't like that none. She's not even fleet. She's admin, part of the skeleton staff before we stood up, and she's afraid a fleet command master chief's going to show up and take her job, so she's got to be a hard ass to prove she's up for it.

Beth thought about that for a moment, then nodded. It made sense.

"What am I doing, gabbing your ear off? I'll be there at your brief on Tuesday."

Brief? What brief? No one told me about that.

"Look, you've got the top rack. You can store your gear under here," she said, pulling open a closet that took up half of the space under her rack.

There were some dirty clothes inside, which Mercy pulled out.

"I'll make some room in the desk for you."

"Thanks," Beth said, then after a moment, "Uh . . . your nose rings. Are they reg?"

Mercy reached up, and in an instant, the nose and lip rings were off. "Can't wear these on flight status, but this is my kingdom here . . . uh, *our* kingdom, so we can do what we want."

That relieved Beth, and she wasn't sure why. Maybe it was because the nose rings were so at odds with what had been driven into her at boot camp, or maybe the Navy's image as portrayed on the holovids.

"And your hair, is that—"

"Real? Real as shit. Do you want to check the cellar to see if it matches the roof?" she asked, starting to pull down the front of her panties.

"No, no, I believe you!"

"Anything else you want to know?" Mercy asked, a sly smile on her face.

There was something, something that had been gnawing at her since she realized Mercy's height.

"Were you OPW, too?"

"What? OPW? Satan's nuts, no. My family hired them, mostly Roma and Trogs, to work our mines, but me? Actually work? Not on your life. Why do you ask?"

"I didn't mean . . . uh . . . well, you're not very tall, and the zaibatsus only hire people like us."

"Oh, my family could have gotten one of the big boys to hire me, I guess, if I'd asked, but not as an OPW. No way . . . oh," she said as it dawned on her. "You were an OPW?"

Beth wished she'd never mentioned it now, but there was nothing to be ashamed of. "Yes, I was."

"They never told us that when they said you were coming. An OPW. No, shit. You're going to have to tell me about that sometime."

Beth's stomach took that moment to rumble again, and Mercy said, "Damn, girl. Did you get chow?"

"No, the master chief tied me up."

"That woman is so blind that she probably forgets to eat herself." She pulled open her closet, rummaged around, and pulled out a packet. "You like Pop-Pop bars? It's a long time 'til midrats."

Navy regs prohibited food items in berthing spaces. Beth didn't know if Mercy was thumbing her nose at those regs or if they just didn't matter as much out here in the fleet. She did like Pop-Pop bars, though, so he held out her hand.

"I've got more where they came from, so just let me know. For now, get a load off your ass," she said, patting a spot on her rack. "I'm about to give you the gouge on everyone you need to know, starting with George, our flight leader."

It took a second for Beth to realize that "George" was Lieutenant Hadley, whom the "Or No Go" had informed her was her flight leader—which meant Mercy was in her four-man flight as well.

"George—Swordfish—is a good guy," she started, eagerness lighting up her eyes as she started to gossip.

She had initially recoiled when she first met her bunkmate, but she was quickly warming up to the woman. Beth was sure they were going to get along just fine.

Chapter 9

"Any saved rounds?" Lieutenant Hadley asked his three flight members.

Beth just wanted to get going. She was excited, and this would be the first time she'd be flying with her flight. She'd gotten in the ten hours the commander wanted in *Tala*, as she'd named her Wasp, the last time with the commander himself, where she chased him through the Navy's Westerman Training Area, matching him maneuver-for-maneuver.

She'd been pretty proud of that until Mercy told her that the CO, for all his vision and leadership, was not the greatest pilot. He didn't really fit into his Wasp, as big as he was, despite modifications made to it, but he insisted on flying like the rest of pilots.

She stole a quick glance at her Wasp, *Tala*. She had agonized for two days on the name, finally settling on the ancient Filipino goddess of the stars and the nighttime sky. She'd never known anything about the ancient gods and goddesses, but once she uploaded the information, the name seemed to fit. "NSP3 Floribeth S. O. Dalisay" was printed on the nose, under which was "Ant."

"Did you get that, Beth?" the lieutenant asked.

"What? Oh, sorry sir."

"I told you to stay back as much as possible. Just get your feet wet this time, OK?"

"Aye-aye, sir," she said.

He'd gone over it enough times in the debrief. Fox Flight was tasked with providing screening from the robin sector, making sure that the main force was not surprised by the enemy. Beth didn't like it—she wanted to be able to mix it up with the bad guys, but she understood his intent. She would basically be screening the screening force, letting Mercy, the lieutenant, or Lieutenant (JG) Kevin Bendick handle any action.

"Well, let's get to it. We launch in twenty."

The four pilots bumped fists together, then turned to their Wasps. Beth restrained herself from pulling down on the crotch of her bright red-and-maroon flight suit—the colors chosen by the CO when the squadron stood up. Her suit was new, and, of course, all the standard sizes were too large for her. This one had been adjusted for her size, but it didn't quite fit right yet. It tended to ride up when she walked, pinching her where she didn't want to be pinched, but she knew there would be eyes on her, checking her out, eyes belonging to crew and pilots, and she didn't need to be seen grabbing at her crotch.

Spaceman Josh Frye was standing at attention by *Tala*, ready to strap her in. He was very junior to be a plane captain, but Senior Chief Garcia had assured her that Frye was up to the task. He did seem competent, but Beth didn't like it. She knew Frye, as an E 3 spaceman, was her plane captain so she could be senior to him, but that wasn't reason enough to push for a change. The minute he screwed up, though . . .

She'd already completed her physical check when the lieutenant had called the flight together, so all she had to do was to get in and run the interior checks.

"I still need this stupid suit adjusted as soon as I get back," she said as she climbed into the cockpit.

"Still riding up on you?" he whispered as he checked her connections.

She was a little embarrassed to admit that to the young man.

Come on, Floribeth. Be professional.

"Yes."

"I'm on it." He looked down at his Check Master, then after a moment, said, "I've got all green, Pilot Dalisay."

"Very well."

She started her checklist. One by one, her telltales turned green. After a minute, she gave Frye a thumbs-up."

"Let's power her up."

A Wasp was made for space flight, but it was capable of landing on a planet, even one with an atmosphere. It could shut down, then be started up under its own power. Both atmosphere and starting up like that, however, contributed to wear and tear, so before a launch, the fighters were powered up by portable initiators.

Frye moved to the initiator, called out, "Powering now," and a surge rushed through the ship, one she could almost feel.

Mercy said it was like a man becoming tumescent—well, her wording was rather cruder—but now that image was stuck in Beth's mind. She smiled, looking over to where her friend was about ready to power up her engine. Mercy looked up, caught her eye, then slowly erected a middle finger as her Wasp powered up.

Girl, have you no shame? Beth thought as she turned back to her display to check the readings.

Beth had already decided that her bunkmate didn't have a trace of shame DNA in her body. There wasn't a mean bone in her body, either. The woman just enjoyed living life to its fullest.

"Hello, Rose," Beth said, addressing her AI. "Wake."

"Hello, Beth. I'm ready."

An operational Wasp's AI was an amazing construct. Ever since the CyberWar almost 200 years ago, AIs had been tightly controlled and limited in their capabilities. The "AI" on her Hummingbird didn't really deserve the term, being little more than a voice-interfaced computer, programmed for a specific decision tree. That was why she'd had to null hers at SG-4021.

Rose was far more capable, but still with limited capabilities. She was not sentient, the IT-types assured her, but sometimes, it was difficult to keep that in mind. She sounded like another person for all practical purposes.

With Rose online, she gave Frye another thumbs-up. She was ready to go. In another 14 minutes, she would be launched.

Fourteen minutes came and went with Beth sitting there. At 20 minutes, the XO, who was not flying today, started going on a screaming rampage, joined by the command master chief. Beth could hear the muffled words inside *Tala*, but she didn't bother to open her external mic.

"Someone's going to get reamed," Mercy passed on an S2S circuit.

"Get off the net, Mercy."

"Don't get your panties in a twist. We're still in the hangar. It's not like anyone else is trying to reach us."

"For all we know, the master chief is listening in to see if we're chatting."

"No, Beth, she isn't. Can't you hear her? I've got to admit, she's got an impressive vocabulary."

"Coming from a gutter mouth like you, that's saying something," Beth said.

"Takes one to know one."

"All hands, launch now set for zero-nine-forty-two," another voice came over the squadron net.

Beth checked the time: a little over seventeen minutes. She settled in to wait.

Forty-three minutes later, the first Wasp launched. It took another nine minutes for Fox Flight's turn. Frye and the other three plane captains stood to the side and saluted as the four Wasps launched.

Holovids and games showed fighters travelling at breakneck speeds in tight formations, almost touching each other. That made for impressive visuals, but it did not reflect reality, particularly in open space. As soon as they launched, the four ships spread out, hundreds of kilometers apart from each other as they aligned to pass through the gate. This would be the chokepoint. This was where an enemy could hit them while they were bunched up. All 44 Wasps would pass through the gate as tightly as possible, then immediately disperse into a more defensible formation. Fox Flight would be almost a megaklick from the main force.

For the gate passage, the choreography was turned over to the Naval Controller's AI. Beth sat back while the AI positioned her, bringing her up to speed and on a course that would get her to the gate at the correct time. When all 44 Wasps were ready, the Naval AI started the process, every fighter converging on the gate like a deck of cards being riffled.

Beth watched, a passenger as *Tala* shot through the gate, then a passenger no longer as she immediately took control, pulling the fighter at close to the maximum Gs to move into position. On her display, the traces of each fighter spread out. The first fighters through the gate were the screening force. The attack force came in last, the 24 ships more tightly bunched as they adjusted course to the anomaly. Beth wished she was with them. She wanted action, not simply to watch events unfold.

Fox Flight had reached its position—now the four pilots had to keep in relative position as the assault force headed into the system. Somewhere ahead, the enemy waited, and the CO wanted to make sure the Stingers stung first.

After the rush of the gate, things quieted down for the next two hours. Her Hummingbird would have taken a good three days to make it into the system, but she was now in a Wasp. Space was huge, however, so even with Wasps, it would take at least three hours for the attack element to reach the source of the anomaly.

"Alpha-four, we've got a reading coming from X-ray-two-two, Yankee-zero-six, Zulu-one-four," Golf-4 passed.

Beth swung around to look, as if she could see over the two megaklicks between Golf and Fox Flights. Golf was flanking the attack force on the opposite side of Fox.

"Rose, how long would it take for us to reach Golf Flight?"

"Approximately two minutes, seventeen seconds."

That doesn't seem right. They're only a couple megaklicks away.

She was about to ask the AI to recalculate before she realized where she'd gone wrong. It would take less if they were already closing, but both flights were slowly separating. A Wasp was highly maneuverable, but at these speeds, it would still take time to come about and change direction.

A moment later, the attack force changed direction, abandoning the original anomaly, and headed to meet the threat. The anomaly could have been a plant or even a natural transmission—now that the enemy had been located, there wasn't a reason to proceed to it.

"OK, Fox Flight, looks like we have rear guard, but keep alert," the lieutenant passed.

"Shit, just our luck," Mercy passed on the S2S. "All this way and no invitation to the dance."

Beth ignored her, instead trying to observe what was happening. Six of the eleven flight teams were maneuvering to envelop the enemy force, building up speed as they closed. The enemy force looked trapped, but it was forming into a Tomiko Defense, which could cause problems cracking it.

"Swordfish, are you getting what I am?" LTJG Bendick asked the lieutenant on the flight net.

With 44 fighters, the pilots used the official call signs to avoid confusion. Within each four-plane flight, however, they used each other's personal call signs. LT Hadley was "Swordfish," LTJG Bendick was "Warthog," Mercy was "Red Devil," and Beth sported her new callsign, "Ant." She wasn't overly happy with it, but no one got to choose their callsign. It was still early enough that it could be changed based on her performance, for good or bad, but she could only hope.

"Rose, slave me to him," Beth ordered, pulling up her own scans. In the top right corner of her helmet display, several more anomalies suddenly appeared. "Most likely probabilities?"

"Nothing over 20%. Do you want me to list them?"

"No, but as soon as one reaches 33%, let me know."

"Fox Flight, orient to x-ray-one, yankee-three-one, zulu-two-five. Full dispersion," Swordfish ordered.

Beth kept running scans, trying to pierce whatever was wrinkling the fabric of space. Anti-surveillance measures were in constant flux, but not many ships could spoof the Navy for long as the AIs acted and counteracted to break through the fog.

Except those aren't run-of-the-mill ships out there, if that's them.

"Now 35% and climbing that those ships are—" Rose started before being cut off by Lieutenant Hadley.

"They're moving too fast. It's them. Prepare for attack, tetrahedron, Ant following. Execute."

The tetrahedron formation was three fighters forward in a triangle, one following at what would be the apex of a pyramid. That maximized firepower to the front but allowed the reserve (Beth in this case) to give support to any of the other three.

Within seconds, as the two forces closed, it became obvious that a total of five enemies faced them, all travelling .2C faster than Fox Flight. They had been building up speed, under heavy cloaking, before they were picked up, which gave them a big advantage.

"We've got help coming," the lieutenant passed. "We just need to keep the bad guys engaged until then. Ready torp salvo on second bogey. Fire in five."

At this range, the torpedoes would probably not be particularly effective, but it could work to disperse the enemy formation. And by focusing on one of them, they could get lucky, taking one of them out.

The enemy had torpedoes, too, and launching them at their craft's higher speed would make them more effective. Beth, hanging 30 kiloklicks behind the lead three, counted down, hoping her wingmen would get theirs off first.

She longed to fire as well, but those weren't her orders. She knew the lieutenant was letting her get her feet wet on this mission, but what better way than to get into the thick of things?

The salvo of three torpedoes took off, accelerating at the max 70G. The enemy force didn't react but kept advancing. At any minute, Beth expected them to fire back.

"Ant, keep them busy. Engage with your laser."

"Roger that," Beth said.

A Wasp configured for ship-to-ship had four weapons systems. The L-40 was a laser, the P-13 a hadron coil-particle beam, the M-51 or 57 torpedo, and the G-21 railgun for close-in fighting.

The laser had almost infinite range and flew at near c speed. It was susceptible to shielding, and the Wasp's laser did not have nearly the power of those on capital ships.

The hadron was a devastating weapon, with the particles building up speed in a kilometer-length cyclotron under the fighter before being shot out. Its weakness was the radiation the process created, the power it required, and its relatively shorter range due to electrostatic bloom.

The torpedoes were the weapon of choice for most engagements. They had a fire-and-forget guidance system that would hone in on the target. One hit would destroy or heavily damage any ship known to man. They were relatively slow, however, and had a somewhat limited range before they lost their maneuverability.

The railgun fired small depleted uranium pellets at hypervelocity speeds that would punch through just about anything. They traveled along a straight line and so could be dodged, so their effective range was limited to a couple hundred klicks, which was spitting distance when considering space combat. In close-combat, such as around a planet or even in atmosphere, the weapon was deadly.

"Engage second target," Beth ordered Rose, using her eye to highlight the blip on her helmet display. "Full power and lock."

The blip's color switched to the red of an active target, and an instant later, a beam of white shot across her display, enhanced for her to follow it. It struck the advancing fighter a moment later, but the enemy kept advancing.

The modern combat laser could cut through almost anything if given enough time. The target could gain time by either shunting most of the beam aside or breaking contact.

Immediately, two of the enemy fired torpedoes, locked on *Tala*. Beth's heart jumped to her throat as adrenaline spiked.

"Give me time to impact!"

"At current closing, twenty-three seconds."

"Damn!"

Her flight's torps would arrive first, but that wouldn't affect the two that were bearing down on her.

"Swordfish, I've got two fish on me."

"You've got time. Keep up the fire for another ten seconds."

"Roger."

Beth gulped as she watched the distance close, almost hoping that the torps would break off to one of the others, then feeling guilty that the thought had crossed her mind. Her display lit up as the other four opposing fighters employed their hadron beams to take out the three Fox Flight torpedoes, which was why they'd waited. It was a calculated risk. A particle beam could destroy any torpedo, but even in the "vacuum" of space, there was dust and micro-particles, and combined with the bloom, a beam weapon lost power with range. Using a hadron beam to knock out an incoming torpedo was a bet that you'd destroy it before it reached you

She couldn't worry about that, though. She had her own game of chicken going, and with seven seconds left, she won that game. Her target swung off and commenced a break maneuver. If Beth could keep locked, her laser would probably get close to breaking through, but that would result in her getting taken out by the enemy torp. She immediately broke as well, spitting out decoys as she ran.

The limit of her compensators, without getting G-Shot, was 53G, and Beth pushed that as she took *Tala* into a series of maneuvers designed to both break the torpedo lock and keep her in position to support the other three.

One of the torpedoes immediately lost lock, honing in on a decoy. The second one, however, stayed on her ass as she pushed *Tala* to her limits. The enemy torp was running much faster than she was. If she just bolted, she'd take it up the stern. Beth had one advantage: because she was slower, she had greater maneuverability.

She swung *Tala* hard over, pulling max Gs. The torp immediately gave chase, closing in to 26.3 klicks on the intercept—ass-puckering close—before the torp shot past, struggling to turn tight enough to hit her.

"You've got two bogeys on your six," Warthog told Mercy.

Beth had been so wrapped up in her own fight to survive that she'd lost the picture. She pulled out her display to see that Swordfish was dead, along with one of the enemy fighters.

Shit! Don't dwell on it—focus!

She saw the two on Mercy's tail, but one was closing with Warthog, and a fourth, Beth's original target, was rejoining the fight.

"I can't shake the fuckers," Mercy shouted over the net as she tried to reverse course and come back to a front aspect.

"I'm coming in," Warthog said, swooping down from the Z-axis.

Trying to escape the enemy torp had taken Beth out of the fight. She kept into her turn to rejoin the other two while she tried to process what she should do next.

"Give me some torpedo firing solutions," she yelled into her helmet.

A moment later, she had four. None gave a high probability of success.

If I can just cut the distance a bit, I can get an aft aspect.

"Red Devil, can you drag it left two, up five, and out three?" Beth asked.

"I'm kinda busy, if you haven't noticed," Mercy said, the tension evident in her voice.

"If you can, then I can support you," Beth passed.

I hope.

"That's a ne—" Warthog started before he was cut off. His blip flashed white, then dulled to gray.

"Fuck, it's just you and me now, sister," Mercy said. "And my shields are taking a pounding."

"Just a little bit longer, and I can fire a torp up their butts."

"Hell, Beth, if you say so. Just hurry up. They're about to burn through."

Beth brought *Tala* from under the battle plane. If this was an old wet-water navy battle, Mercy was a destroyer with two cruisers on her, while *Tala* was a submarine, maneuvering to fire a salvo of torpedoes at the cruisers. She just had to get into range.

She checked the position of the other two fighters. Her original target was looping back to get into the fight, and the one that had just taken out Bendick was angling on a converging course with Mercy. None of them seemed to be paying any attention to her.

Your mistake, suckas!

She had Rose continually calculating firing solutions, waiting for the right moment. When the probability of a hit reached 30%, she almost went for it, but she wanted the element of surprise, and a missed shot would remind them that she was a threat. She had to take out the two on Mercy for them to have a chance with the remaining two.

They really should be paying attention to me . . .

A flashing white light on her display took her attention away from the firing solutions. She glanced at it.

Mother of God! The torpedo!

The torpedo she'd dodged had come around, and with Beth's change of course, she'd become a sitting duck. Rose was a highly developed AI, but by keeping her "consciousness" on continual firing solutions, that had left legacy displays for all other functions—such as incoming threats.

She fired her two torpedoes and tried to "dive under" the incoming torp, but she knew she was out of time. The enemy torpedo hit, and *Tala* went dark.

Chapter 10

"I thought you were supposed to be God's gift to the Navy," Warrant Officer Two Taurus Nicolescu said as Beth and Mercy headed for the ready room. "Pretty piss-poor performance, if you ask me."

Taurus—who'd unsurprisingly been given the callsign "Bull"—was one of the squadron's three warrant officers, former enlisted pilots who'd been first class petty officers and had put in three years as single-seat pilots. The idea of enlisted-to-warrant pilots went back a long way, at least as far as the old American Army. The concept had been resurrected as a compromise between the old guard, who still thought all fighter and attack pilots should be commissioned officers, and the new who'd pushed for the change.

Technically, Beth was a "probationary" pilot. She wouldn't shuck off the probationary status until, and if, she became a warrant officer.

Which wasn't a sure thing after her performance in the exercise.

"And you are, Bull? God's gift?" Mercy said, grabbing Beth by the arm and pulling her past the man.

"Watch it, Hamlin," Nicolescu said.

"Yeah, yeah, I know. You're the high and mighty O, while me and Beth here are just dumb enlisted peons."

"Jeez, Mercy! Be careful," Beth whispered as they got out earshot.

Normal naval etiquette was somewhat lax in fighter squadrons, far more so than in a ship, or, God help it, in the

Marines. Among the pilots themselves, it was even more casual, but she thought Mercy was pushing the limits, and she didn't want her friend to get into trouble.

"He can eat me. 'Bull' is appropriate for him; he flies like the proverbial bull in a china shop. The asshole's got no touch."

Beth didn't know enough about the man to comment. He'd been one of about a dozen or so who seemed to resent her presence. Most of her squadron mates had seemed to be either welcoming or neutral, but those dozen went out of their way to exclude her.

She thought it was going to get worse now, too. Lieutenant Hadley had already reamed her out, listing all the mistakes she'd made. Beth had bristled at some of his charges, but she'd kept it inside. He'd been the one who'd ordered her to stay back, after all, so those "mistakes" were on him. The fact of the matter, however, was that she'd made three fatal mistakes. The first was forgetting the torpedo she'd dodged. The second was forgetting that Rose, for all her programmed personality, was still a limited AI, and when she'd put her on the task to continually update the firing solutions, she could only put the torpedo warning up on the display.

The third was the most egregious. She'd been too cautious. She'd been waiting for the perfect shot, something that put Mercy at risk and had ended up with Beth being taken out of the exercise.

As a commercial scout pilot, deliberate and well-thought-out decisions were what was required. A fighter pilot had to have that confidence and ability to make quick decisions if they were going to be effective. Others in the Navy usually considered them brash, but that's the type of person who was needed.

And ever since she sat there in her "dead" fighter, going over every step of the fight, she wondered if she didn't have what it took. The warrant officer was being a dick, but what he'd said fed into her doubts.

The two entered the ready room, moving to the far-right bulkhead, where as junior enlisted, they would stand in the overpacked room. Most of the red force was already in place. These were some of the best pilots in the Navy, now assigned to the OPFOR to put squadrons through their paces. This had been the first "battle" between the two squadrons with three more to go before the Stingers were certified as combat-ready.

One of the red pilots caught Beth's eyes, then smiled and pointed his hand like a pistol and mimicked firing it at her. She knew in an instant that he was the one who'd taken her out. With all the grace she could muster, she nodded back at him.

Next time, buddy!

Technically, the Stingers had "won" the engagement, but the mood among the squadron was sober while the red force pilots were in good spirits. With more and better fighters, the Stingers should have done much better. Aside from Beth, the lieutenant, and Warthog, the squadron had lost 16 of the 44 Wasps. It could easily have been 17, but Beth's last-gasp firing of her torpedoes made the two red force Wasps react just enough for Mercy to keep them at bay until Delta Flight arrived.

"Attention on deck!" someone shouted as seated pilots rose to their feet.

Rear Admiral Kyra Rubenstein entered the ready room, followed by a couple of captains and a posse of lower-ranking officers. She reached the empty front rank of seats, then said, "At ease. We've got a lot to go over today, so let's get going."

The admiral was the sector operations officer, and she had decided on a hands-on approach while the squadron went through certification. Unlike the CO, she had never been a pilot, instead commanding the larger ships where her GT height wasn't an issue. If the quick look she gave the CO as she took her seat was any indication, she didn't think he should be in the cockpit as well.

One of the captains accompanying her continued to the podium, then said, "As the admiral has said, we've got a lot to cover here today, so get yourself comfortable."

There was a low murmur of laughs.

"We're going to start with an overview of the exercise, then go into details on each engagement with deep dives into Bravo and Fox Flights . . ."

Oh, shit. This isn't going to be good, Beth realized as she prepared herself for a long and very uncomfortable afternoon.

Chapter 11

"So, you like being a pilot and all?" Spaceman Apprentice Mikel Botha asked as he scrubbed the urinal in front of him.

Beth turned her head to him and thought for a moment, trying to pick the right wording. "We've all got jobs to do, Mikel. Like this," she said, pointing her brush at the urinal she was cleaning.

She did feel special, being a pilot, but it wouldn't do her much good with her dwindling reputation in the station if she sounded arrogant. And what she'd said was true. For all the good being a pilot did here, the command master chief could still assign her to lead the three-person working party to clean the heads.

"I know, but, you wear the blue, just like other pilots," he said, pointing at her work coveralls.

"And what am I doing now? Cleaning pissers, just like you."

Botha laughed, then said, "I guess you're right at that."

"That's me, petty officer in charge of heads," she said.

Another petty officer came in, saw the two, and shrugged, unsealing his overalls.

"Hey, we're cleaning in here," Beth said.

"And I'm pissing. So what?"

"So what? This head's secured until we're done, that's what. You didn't see the sign?"

The petty officer already had his hand inside his overalls, but he rolled his eyes, said, "It ain't going to make any difference," and left.

Beth knew she could have let it go, but she didn't want to watch—and listen—to him piss, and she wasn't happy she was even in this position. This had been the sixth time she'd been assigned to a head-cleaning working party. The master chief was simply exerting her authority over her, making sure Beth knew, pilot or not, that she owned her.

Heck, she didn't even *use* a urinal, and here she was, getting to know more about them than she wanted. It was mind-boggling that after centuries of amazing technological advantages, urinals hadn't changed much, and they still needed manual cleaning. Mercy said there had to be a high-tech lab somewhere that had developed a pisser that kept guys from dripping on the deck, but the Navy brass suppressed it so that they could have something to assign sailors to do.

"How're you doing in there, Leung?" she called out to the sailor cleaning the shitters on the other side of the sinks.

"I'm OK."

"We're about done out here, so we'll be there in a few."

Spaceman Recruit Glorya Tantus Leung was a quiet, unassuming sailor. She'd been busted down from E3 to E1 for sucker-punching her petty officer, dropping him like a ton of bricks. She could have been court-martialed, but it had been handled with captain's mast. She'd also been fined and assigned additional duty, which was why she was with Beth cleaning heads, and had been with her each time Beth had been given the duty. She knew there was more to the sailor's story, and she was curious as to what really went down, but the sailor kept to herself.

She cleaned the last urinal in the line, then dumped the brush in her bucket and stood up, knees creaking. She didn't have to do the cleaning herself. As the petty officer in charge, she was not being punished, and she could stand back and just watch—"supervising." She knew that was what most others did, but with only three of them, the task would get done a lot quicker if she pitched in. Beth might be a petty officer, and a pilot at that, but while she resented the master chief's harassment, she didn't feel she was "above" anyone else. If the heads needed to be cleaned, then she was going to help get it done.

She was just about to join Leung in the shitters when the announcement over the 1MC said, "All Stinger pilots, report to the ready room."

Beth whipped off her gloves and dumped them into the disposal.

"Botha, you're in charge now. Finish up this head, then report back to your division."

"What about the other two?"

"If the command master chief wants them cleaned, she can come get me after I find out what's up."

She briefly considered changing into a new set of overalls, but she didn't want to wait to find out what was going on. It could be something as routine as signing a new Next of Kin doc, but something in her gut told her it was something else—something big.

She ran down the passage to find out.

Chapter 12

Beth's instincts had been right. Less than a week after certification, the squadron had a hot mission—reconnaissance, but still hot.

The surveillance spooks had collected several hints of what could have been evidence of an alien presence: tiny ripples in space that had no other known explanation. The three most likely locations were selected, and three eight-Wasp flights were going to recon the areas, loaded down with the best surveillance instruments available. This was not a combat mission. Each Wasp would be armed, of course, and free to implement full capabilities, to include G-Shot, if it became necessary. But the intent was to get in, find out what was there, and get out.

Each eight-Wasp flight would transit, along with another four-Wasp flight and a monitor, through three gates, making a round-about route to the target gate. While the eight Wasps entered the target systems, four more and the big monitor would guard the gate, ready to destroy it should it be threatened—even if there were still fighters on the other side. No aliens would be allowed through.

What surprised Beth, though, was that Fox Flight was assigned to one of the missions. After the brutal debrief of her first mission, where their actions had been stripped bare, Fox Flight had been given support-type roles for the next three missions against the OPFOR. Yet here they were, not only merged with Delta Flight, but with Lieutenant Hadley in command.

"He must have blown the CO to get us here," Mercy had said as they got out of their overalls and donned their flight suits.

Beth wouldn't have cared what he'd done—she just wanted vindication. She knew that some of her fellow pilots had decided she was out of her league, a politically-correct addition to the squadron, and as such, a dangerous wingman. Others (she hoped) had not made up their minds, and she wanted to prove herself to them. She couldn't do that by being in the rear with the gear but instead had to be at the tip of the spear.

"Better not fuck up, Ant," Warrant Officer Nicolescu passed on the S2S. "I want to get back in one piece."

And that was the one bad thing about the mission. Nicolescu was in Delta Flight, and so now they were together, designated "Purple Flight."

The pairing of Delta and Fox was not accidental. Delta was commanded by Tuna, a mustang lieutenant who'd made it up to chief before accepting a commission. With Bull and Ranger, a Petty Officer First Class, and Uncle, another lieutenant, this was the most experienced flight where the flight leader would be junior to the lieutenant. The CO was giving him—and Fox—a chance, but paired them with another strong, experienced flight.

Beth ignored Nicolescu. She wasn't going to give him the satisfaction of a response. They wouldn't be actually flying together, anyway. Delta and Fox Flights might be under one command, but they would be flying as separate maneuver elements.

"Kick some ass, OK?" Josh asked as he checked the weapons station connections.

"We're just going there to look around. You know that."

"Yeah, I know what they said, but I don't think the aliens heard that."

Josh had turned out to be a very capable plane captain. Senior Chief Garcia had done her a solid with him. He seemed to intuitively understand what *Tala* needed, and she thought he was better than any of the others, no matter their experience level.

"Just make sure my guns are ready, young spaceman."

"Up and ready, oh exalted Petty Officer Third Class Floribeth Salinas O'Shea Dalisay," he said, coming to an exaggerated position of attention, a palm-forward salute.

Beth just rolled her eyes. Josh had a weird sense of humor, no doubt about it, but she wouldn't trade him for anyone else.

The launch warning came, and it was time to get to the rails. All eight Wasps lined up, with the gate drone on the far side. The other four Wasps had already launched, and the Third Fleet monitor should already be on station. Josh and the other plane captains got into position, ready to send them off.

Beth half-expected the lieutenant to give them one last pep talk, but evidently, even he must have figured they'd had enough. Each pilot sat alone in silence. Beth felt her nerves rising.

"Purple Flight, are you green for launch?" the CAT officer finally asked over the net.

"Roger, we're green, CAT."

"Purple is green," Mercy said with a laugh on their S2S.

"Understand green. Standby, launch in five . . . four . . . three . . . two . . . one!"

Josh and the other plane captains were a blur as each Wasp shot down the rails, separated by less than a second in time, but tens of kilometers of distance that opened up farther as the NTC guided them off the station and towards the gate arrays.

For all the excitement of the launch, it would take most of a day to transit through the gates, building up speed as they went. Within half-an-hour, Beth was bored, and one big minus when comparing a Wasp with a Hummingbird was that the Wasp didn't have an entertainment console. Beth popped in her personal earbud, then tried to relax and listen to music.

At least no slime, she told herself like she did every time she pulled down her tubes. She had some low-particulate snacks like jerky and chocolate, but the tubes held up to six liquids, two being protein shakes. They weren't great, but anything was pretty good compared to slime.

To her surprise, there was a handwritten note attached to Tube 6 that said, "Try me."

Curious, she took a tentative sip—it was Coke!

You son-of-a-bitch, Josh!

Carbonated beverages were a no-go aboard a Wasp, and even if smuggled on, they quickly lost their fizz. But this was just great, just like normal.

Josh had broken regs to get her the Coke, and she was required to report him, but there was no way that was going to happen. She took another long sip, then pushed the tube shelf back up. She wanted to parcel it out for the entire trip, and she still had hours to go.

****

"Scans on as soon as you pass the gate," Lieutenant Hadley reminded them as they lined up for the final approach.

This is it. Get it together, Floribeth.

Beth was both excited and nervous—excited that she was finally on her first real mission, but nervous that she'd screw up. While she'd performed OK on the last three exercises—nothing extraordinary, but nothing negative, either—the ghost of the first mission was still haunting her. It wasn't so much that fact that she'd been "killed" but that she'd let down her fellow pilots.

"Approaching gate in twenty seconds," Rose told her.

She'd reset her settings on her AI. Rose now monitored all data streams, then announced what she prioritized as the most important, even if asked a specific question or given a specific task.

Beth kissed her cross, then held her breath, the last a weird habit she'd picked up when entering a gate, and a moment later, *Tala* shot into SG-9222, a binary system on the far side of the galaxy. She flipped on her scans, the primary being a Case densitometer. Case made mining equipment, and the densitometer was one of their commercial scanners, modified for usage with a Wasp. In addition to the normal scanners on a Wasp, each of the eight in the flight had an extra scanner in an attempt to cover all the bases. The science types gave it a low probability of being useful, and so, of course, it had been installed on the junior-most pilot's fighter.

It seemed like they were right. They were still quite far out, but the densitometer was only getting vague readings on potential mineral deposits.

"Return gate emplaced and coordinates locked," Rose said.

Beth barely paid attention to the report. She noted that the drone that had followed the fighters had given them their way back, but since changing the AI's settings, Rose's pseudo-personality had taken a hit.

"I'm getting something, but I don't know what," Ranger passed.

Beth *did* pay attention to that.

"What're you getting, Ranger? And on which system?" the lieutenant asked.

"On the Six-F. I'm running the results through my AI now."

Am I the only one to name my AI? Beth wondered for a moment. Mercy had given her a ration of shit when she'd told her she'd named Rose, but in every holovid, the AIs, real or fictional, always had cool names.

"I've got nothing concrete, and it could be internal static, but my gut tells me this could be something. Sending over the azimuth now."

There was a pregnant pause, and Beth knew that seven pilots were waiting for Swordfish's decision.

Are they out there?

"Delta Flight, adjust course toward the possible source. Fox, continue on present course. Ranger, keep your Six-F on whatever it might be."

The original plan was for both flights to conduct flybys of the system's two stars, never slowing down as Beth had done in her Hummingbird, but using a gravity assist trajectory to whip around each star and head back to the gate. What might take three or four days in a scout would take the fighters a little over eight hours—although that also took into account the fact that the gate had been opened well within the system, not outside, as they were with the various exploration corps.

"Of course, the fucking Delta dicks get the glory," Mercy passed on the S2S.

"We don't know that it's anything," Beth said.

She understood Mercy's sentiments, though. She might have almost bought the farm the last time she encountered one of the aliens, but she was in a Wasp this time, and not alone. She'd sure like to meet them again from a position of power.

"And we don't know that it's not, either."

"It's not like we'll be that far apart, so if it is them, we're just a shout away."

Which was true. The two stars were an extremely tight binary orbiting each other at six AU. As they took advantage of the stars' gravitational pull, the two flights would be about an hour apart.

"Fox Flight, I'm changing our course," the lieutenant passed. "You've got the new one now."

Beth pulled up the trajectory on her display. He'd obviously been considering the same time factors that she had. Their previous course had them slinging around the star from the opposite side of the other star. Now, the course had them slinging around from the inside. The lieutenant had just cut the response time in half, should Delta get into trouble.

For the next hour, the eight ships hurtled towards the two stars at max Gs, building up more speed. *Tala's* scanners weren't showing anything out of the ordinary, and she kept glancing at Ranger's blip on her helmet display, wondering what he was getting. When Delta went under 20 minutes before beginning their gravity assist slingshot (and Fox was at 32 minutes), Beth decided that Ranger's reading was just a hiccup, an anomaly.

And then all hell broke loose.

As if coming out from behind a curtain, first five bogeys appeared on her display, identified by most of *Tala's* scanners.

"Tally five," Tuna said in a calm voice. A moment later, seven more popped up, and Tuna said, "Correction, tally twelve." All 12 were on the other side of Delta and heading for an intercept.

Purple Flight's orders were to avoid engagement. This was a recon mission, not an assault mission. Already, there was data streaming in that would give the analysts a huge boost in figuring out just what the aliens were.

"Break, break . . . hold that," the lieutenant started.

The orders had been that if there were aliens in the system, the flight would break contact. However, this close to the stars, breaking contact immediately might not be the quickest way to get back to the gate. Breaking before reaching the stars would mean fighting the stars' gravity, much like Beth in the *Lily* had planned to do before the situation got away from her. It might be the case that continuing forward, then using the stars' gravity well to sling around would be quicker—if the alien ships were far enough away to allow for that.

"Rose, what is the intercept to Delta Flight given the alien ships and keeping the current course?"

The lieutenant would be running the numbers, too, and he wouldn't be asking her, but she wanted to know the answer.

"Thirty-two minutes, fourteen seconds."

What about any weapons they have? I know they've got torpedoes. How far can they reach?

"OK, Purple, continue on present course with the gravity assist. Weapons free, but I don't have to remind, you, we fire only if fired upon."

"Fuck that. If they look at me funny, I'm lighting them up," Mercy passed on the S2S. "Don't like running," she added quietly.

"Neither do I, but you heard Swordfish."

This was a historic moment, what could be the first-ever clash between the Navy of Humankind and an alien force, and the Navy was running. It made strategic sense, but that didn't mean it didn't sting.

Beth rearranged her display to show the two stars, the eight friendlies, and the twelve aliens, all with timers to various points. It looked like Fox Flight would reach their star with a good time cushion, but Delta's window would be much tighter. They might have to take a G-Shot and speed up.

No pilot wanted a G-Shot. It did allow for the human body to survive a fighter's maximum Gs, but it was good for only a limited amount of time before it became fatal, and once initiated, it tore the body up, requiring several weeks of convalescence and creating complications that surfaced later in life.

Plus, it evidently hurt like hell.

"Don't focus on Delta," the lieutenant passed to Fox Flight. "We don't need any surprises on our side."

Beth grimaced. She'd been doing exactly that. She split her helmet display so she could monitor all of the scanning being done. Still, she couldn't help but watch the numbers as the forces closed.

"Warthog, you got anything at all?" the lieutenant asked.

LTJG Bendick had a broadcast pod on his Wasp that was continually ranging different types of spectrums, broadcasting in verbal and binary languages. The forces were close enough for some of those signals to reach the aliens.

"Nothing that my AI can interpret, but there might be something."

There was a long pause, then the lieutenant passed, "You've got the priority on the gate. Make sure your comms pod is recovered. Red Devil and Ant, make sure Warthog gets through, no matter what."

"Aye, aye," Mercy and Beth chimed, then Mercy added on the S2S, "What's that about? What's *he* going to be doing?"

It did seem to be an odd order, but Beth quickly forgot about it as Delta started slinging around their star. The aliens were still closing, but it looked like with the extra speed in the gravity assist, the flight would be able to outrun the bad guys back to the gate.

That was assuming the aliens didn't change their course or speed, which, of course, they did.

The lead five immediately sped up, pulling some remarkably high G's, and five smaller blips appeared, shooting out ahead.

"Torpedoes!" Beth passed instinctively, but needlessly.

"Brilliant powers of observation, Ant," Nicolescu said on the S2S. "Now how about getting off the fucking net so we can fight?"

Chagrined, Beth shut up, listening as Tuna ordered seeker mines and torpedoes of their own.

"Fox, engage with lasers as I designate, but keep on present course," Lieutenant Hadley passed.

The distance between Fox and the aliens was at the limit of the torpedo's range. The torps would keep flying forever, but they could only maneuver for a limited amount of time. The lasers, however, had almost unlimited range.

One of the alien ships lit up in flashing yellow—this was her target. Beth locked on and fired.

What the holovids never got right was the wait between firing and hitting the target, even with lasers and particle beams. Rose continued to track the target's path, taking into account that the position of the image on Beth's display lagged the actual position, then created a probability cone on where it should be by the time the laser reached it. It was a constant game of very high-level math, math that didn't even exist until a few hundred years ago. Any military-grade laser could take out a fly's nuts at a million klicks—the problem was figuring out where the fly would be when the beam got there.

Beth held her breath, expecting to see some sort of reaction when she was on target, then let it out with a "Whoop!" when her target jinked. She'd either hit or at least put the fear of God into it. Either way, that should help out Delta, which slung around their star, soon to be out of Fox's sight until both emerged on the other side of their respective stars and were heading back to the gate.

LTJG Bendix's target also jinked, but the remaining three kept to their courses. From behind and below the system's orbital plane, the other seven continued to close the distance.

"Ready torps," the lieutenant passed. "Second group of aliens."

As Fox started into its gravity assist, the star would block their fire, so the self-guiding torpedoes were their only option. The range was still on the outer edge, but it was better than nothing.

Beth acknowledged her two targets, armed the trigger, then poised, finger over the firing button, waiting for the order. Each second brought the forces closer together, but they didn't want to get too far into the star's gravity well before firing.

She wished she could hear what was going on with Delta, but she was not on their flight net. As the Purple Flight commander, the lieutenant could listen in, but if he was, he wasn't passing anything to the other three in Fox.

"Stand by for torpedoes . . . fire!"

Beth pushed the button, one of the few mechanical controls in her Wasp. Two of her three torpedoes shot out, then adjusted their courses for the aliens. She craned her head around, but they were already out of sight as they flew across the void.

Just as Delta passed behind their star, her display lit up with pink lines, emanating from the group of seven bogeys.

Pink?

"Rose, what are the pink lines?"

"Unknown source. The probability is that they represent a yet-unknown energy weapon."

"Just fucking great," Mercy broke in on the S2S. "You getting this, Beth?"

"Sure am. What are they?"

"No freaking clue. That's why they're 'unknown.' Can't be good, though."

One of Delta ships' blip winked out. It was Nicolescu's.

"Shit!" Mercy said, before being cut off by the lieutenant saying, "Keep on course."

Beth felt a sudden surge of nausea. She'd known being a Wasp pilot was a dangerous job, but that was an abstract—until now. Bull was gone, just like that.

And then they were whipping around their star, building up frightening speed. Beth's mind was in a daze while she fought to keep from throwing up.

They reached the point when they started to pull out of the orbit, and Beth forced herself to focus. She had to be in the here and now.

"Remember, Kevin, you've got to get the comms pod back. Nothing gets in your way. Red Devil and Ant, protect his ass!" the lieutenant passed.

Something was up, and Beth didn't know what. She pulled up the lieutenant on her display, wondering if there was something wrong with his Wasp. But no, his readings were fine. She was just about to cut away from the fighter when she realized the Wasp wasn't heading out. It was still in the grav assist orbit.

"You're drifting, Swordfish," she passed on the S2S.

Cutting a course too tight, especially at these speeds when mistakes were more difficult to correct, could have deadly consequences. Plummeting into the star was more than a real possibility.

"Lieutenant, you're deviating."

"Just keep your course, Ant."

"But . . ." she started before she understood.

He's going to support Delta.

At the moment, Delta and Fox were whipping around to head to the gate. If the lieutenant kept the gravity assist and headed for the other star, he'd be heading in the wrong direction. His only options would be to make a huge loop and try and make it back to the gate or whip around Delta's star.

Neither option was optimal. Looping around would take time, time he might not have. Using Delta's star for a gravity assist would entail him heading right at the alien ships first.

Her hands were moving before her brain had actually made the decision. She pulled in her course as well. She was too late to be on the lieutenant's tail, but she should be keeping within range of where she could support him.

Bendix had already started to pull out of the orbit to head to the gate, followed a moment later by Mercy.

"Beth, what the hell are you and Swordfish doing?"

"Delta needs support."

"Fuck! Ok, I'm coming, too."

"Too late. You're too far out now. And you heard the Swordfish. You gotta get Warthog through the gate."

"Ant! What are you doing?" the lieutenant passed, his voice breaking in anger.

"I'm coming with you, sir."

"I gave you a direct order."

"Sorry about that, but you know I'm really a civilian at heart, not much for discipline and such."

"Damn it! Take another orbit and follow the other two."

"Not going to happen, sir," she said.

She switched to the S2S and asked, "Mercy?"

"I'm heading to the gate," her friend said in a subdued voice. "Satan's nuts, just fucking make it back, OK?"

"You've got it."

And then *Tala* was emerging from the star. To her left, the second star shone brightly. Beth had to bring the fighter around with a long way to catch up to the lieutenant.

"Maybe you really aren't Navy material, Ant," the lieutenant passed on the S2S, making Beth's heart fall. "But I'm glad you're here. Let's kick some ass, OK?"

"Roger that."

"Kicking the G-Shot," Ranger passed. "Don't know how much good it's going to do."

The lieutenant must have tied me into the Delta net.

She wasn't sure why, if Ranger and . . .

Hell, it's only Ranger and Uncle left.

. . . if those two were going to kick the G-Shot, why wasn't it going to do any good?

"Understood. Godspeed," Swordfish said.

"Ant, Tuna and Bull are gone. Ranger and Uncle have both been hit, their fighters damaged. They don't know if the ships will reach max Gs. One bogey was destroyed by a mine, but four are closing fast. I'm going to try and give them a little breathing room. I want you to fire your last torp, then use your hadron before you break contact. Understood?"

"Roger that. Understood."

"And no hero stuff, hear me?"

"No hero stuff, roger."

Like you aren't doing that?

Beth was pulling her Wasp around, trying to get into position to support the lieutenant. The four enemy bogies were approaching the star, and it wouldn't be long before they reached it and had a clear line-of-sight to the two Delta Wasps.

The seven—no, six other bogies were lagging behind. One of them was gone, she hoped to a Navy torpedo. Pink lines of whatever weapons they had were still lighting up Beth's display, but not with as heavy a salvo as before.

Both Ranger and Uncle kicked their G-Shots, but their Wasps didn't accelerate. With the shots invading their systems, they quit speaking, and the net became quiet. Beth tried not to imagine what they were going through—and evidently needlessly. Their ships were damaged and couldn't accelerate, with four bogies bearing down on them.

"Kevin, get two tugs. I'm not sure Uncle or Ranger are going to be able to line up for the gate."

"What about you?" Bendick asked. "You and Ant."

"I'm going to try and get the bogies off of their asses. Ant's going to give me some support, then hightail it back to you. Don't wait if you have to destroy the gate."

"Roger that."

"Sorry about that, Ant, but . . ."

"Understand completely."

She did understand, but that didn't stop the wave of fear that washed over her. This could, probably would, be it. She didn't expect to make it back. She'd been very lucky the first time, and she'd probably used up all the luck she had. Her left hand started trembling.

She popped the drink tube into the base of her helmet and took a long drink of Coke, the cold fizziness breaking her mood, and getting rid of the sourness in her mouth.

Thanks, Josh.

She shook her head once, then leaned forward in the cockpit. It was time to get down to business.

****

"Get some, Swordfish!" Beth yelled as the lieutenant swooped into battle, scoring his first kill.

He'd hit the four bogies as soon as they emerged from behind the star with his remaining torpedoes and his Hadron. It was the particle beam that had destroyed one of the bogies, and he was now sweeping it across the other three.

Beth launched her remaining torpedo—they hadn't seemed to be overly effective, but it wasn't doing her any good sitting in its cradle. Now it was time to see what she could do with her hadron.

She was still pretty far out, her looping correction to join the lieutenant had taken her much longer to travel. Still, she should be putting a lot of energy on her targets. The problem was that particle beams traveled close to C, but never reached them, so the time for the beams to travel was longer. The weapons systems compensated by spreading the beam out for longer shots, which allowed for easier targeting, but less power on the target itself. Beth could tell she was scoring hits, but she was not getting kills.

Just let me get closer.

Alarms blared out for a moment, and Beth's heart jumped. She'd had a near-miss with one of the pink beams of the six ships. She still didn't know what they were, but with the formation hanging back and seemingly relying on them, she was pretty sure she didn't want to get hit with one.

One of the three bogies had dropped below the orbital plane as it started to come back to the lieutenant, so, Beth trained her gun on it. Half way through its arc, it broke off.

"Thanks, Ant," the lieutenant said. "And that lets me . . . take that, bastard!"

Navy communications were instantaneous with twinned comm sets, but Beth had to wait to see what he was talking about, screaming her warrior cry when she saw. He'd just scored another kill.

Maybe we're going to get out of here alive?

The hope was short-lived. Just seconds later, the lieutenant was hit, most of his readings dropping to zero.

"Swordfish, are you OK?"

"Ant, I'm hit. Trying to affect repairs."

"How bad is it?"

"Ant, do you read me?"

"I read you, Swordfish. How bad is your fighter?"

"Ant? Ant? Shit, can she even hear me? Ant? If you can read me, I'm in bad shape. I think my core is cracked . . ."

Which meant his cockpit would be getting flooded with gamma particles.

"I'm going to try a reboot, but . . . look, stay with Uncle and Ranger. Get them back, OK?"

"I'm not going to leave you!" she shouted knowing he couldn't hear.

Both remaining bogies were coming back to finish him off. Anger surged through her, replacing everything else. To her very core, she wanted to rend and destroy whatever those things were out there.

She fired her hadron again, but she was still too far out for the cannon to have much effect.

Fuck it!

She pulled off the cover next to her head, turned the knob, then pulled. Immediately, molten fire poured into her veins and arteries, burning her up from the inside. She screamed in agony as the G-shot filled her body, giving it support, the screams choking off as oxygenated fluid filled her lungs to keep them from collapsing. Her arms were heavy, and she switched to back to verbal commands, which seemed counter-intuitive, since she could barely speak—but the throat mic was designed to pick up her subvocalizations.

"Max G," she managed to form with her voice box and throat muscles, and *Tala* leaped to obey.

The compensators screamed in protest, but they couldn't keep her alive without the G-shot. While her body slowed down, four injections into her brain kept her functioning. It wasn't enough to be able to sustain 80Gs—she had to be able to fight.

Tala closed the gap, and Beth increased power to her forward shields and then started firing five-second bursts of the hadron as the bogies continued to close in on the lieutenant.

"Ant, is Swordfish . . ." she heard Bendick pass, but she ignored whatever he had to ask. It took too much effort to keep focused on the enemy.

She took a hit from one of the enemy weapons, all of her alarms going off at once, but somehow, *Tala* held together despite the punishment. Another hit rattled her fighter, but she kept flying.

Thank you, Josh, she thought, grateful for his tireless work keeping *Tala* in top condition.

The next blast of her hadron connected. The bogie simply came apart as the tiny particles penetrated the ship— and a moment later, the shot the bogie had gotten off before it was destroyed hit her.

This time, she wasn't so lucky. Her lower weapons pod was damaged—the pod with the hadron and laser. With no laser, no hadron, and no more torpedoes, Beth was out of major weapons, and the lieutenant was a sitting duck for the last bogie.

But Beth and *Tala* were closing fast, very fast. With thoughts of physically ramming the enemy ship, she shifted her course to intercept.

Wait a minute, girl. Think. Fight the G-shot!

She did have one more weapon: her rail gun. It might not be designed for long-range ship-to-ship combat, but it could still get the job done. It was accurate only to a hundred or two hundred klicks, which meant she had to get in close.

With a supreme effort of will, she checked the status. To her relief, it was up. She brought it online, then watched as the distance closed. She felt like a Zulu warrior, armed with a spear, facing a fleet Marine in full combat armor. Still, a spear would kill if it hit the target.

The enemy bogie fired on the lieutenant, and only then seemed to realize that an avenging angel was on its ass. Beth croaked out a shout as she opened the rail gun, and five thousand tiny pellets, each traveling at .93 C, crossed the distance between them. Whether one of the depleted uranium rounds or a dozen hit, it didn't matter. At that velocity, the results were catastrophic, and the enemy ship turned into just so much space dust.

The G-shot was taking its toll as Beth zoomed past. She'd been under it too long already, and she barely managed to hit the purge and start to slow the ship down.

"Way to go, sister," Mercy passed as the rebound meds kicked in, rendering the universe a fuzzy dream.

Chapter 13

"Beth, wake up," Mercy said.

"No, ten more minutes."

"You've got to wake up now."

"I feel like crap."

"I know you do, honey, but you've really got to get up. We're not going to be able to keep the gate open after Uncle and Ranger make it."

Gate? What's she talking about?

As her mind cut through the fog, she remembered. The mission, the fight . . . the lieutenant!

"Where's Swordfish?" she mumbled as she forced her eyes open.

Her body was still sluggish, but her mind was snapping to.

"He didn't make it. But he got two of the bastards. You, too."

She felt a hollowness in her heart—not anger, not sorrow, just hollowness. She knew the rebound meds were affecting her emotions and she would grieve later.

"And the others? The other seven?" she asked, pulling up her display.

"Tuna got one with a torpedo, and the others hung back."

"I think they're like gunships, there for support," Beth said.

"Maybe, but listen, Beth, no time for that. You're on a course for deep space, and you've got to get turned around. Are you up for that?"

It took her a moment to make sense of Mercy's words. She finally realized that if she didn't take action, she could be left flying out of this system forever, a system with at least six enemy ships. The thought didn't bother her too much, and it just seemed like too much effort to start turning *Tala* around. She stared at her display, wondering what it would be like to just keep on going. There was something else on her display, just flying up ahead of her. She could join that.

Wait, what is that?

It was inert, but moving fast, and not in an orbit around the binary stars.

"Rose, run a reverse azimuth on the object," she said, almost forgetting to highlight it.

The AI plotted a course that led back to the binary star around which Delta slingshotted.

"I've think I've found Bull," she said, slurring the words as she tried to stay alert.

"Bull's dead, honey. Just make your course change and come back."

"No, I really think it's him."

There was a delay, then Bendick came on the net and said, "That tracks, Ant. But Bull's dead. He was hit early in the fight. You need to come back now."

"How do you know he's dead?" she asked, feeling frustrated.

"His Wasp's got no power. Nothing."

"But there's no debris. It's one solid mass."

"How can you tell that, Ant? You're too far away."

Beth cackled like a crazy woman, then said, "I've got 55 missions analyzing systems. I know how to read the data."

There was silence for a moment, which hopefully meant Mercy and Bendick were talking it over. Neither Ranger nor Uncle would be much good if they were in the same state as she was.

It was an effort to speak aloud, so she sub-vocalized and told Rose to adjust course to match that of the object's.

"Beth, there's no way Bull's alive, and if you don't come back now, you're going to be stuck here. And you've kicked G-Shot, for fuck's sake—you need to get to sickbay."

Beth smiled. It felt good to have a friend who cared. And Bull wasn't her friend. But he was a wingman. She had no choice.

"Beth, you've changed course. What are you doing?"

Beth turned down the sound. It was easier to just sit there in silence, not moving.

****

Bull's Wasp was in visual range, less than 600 meters just ahead. Beth ceded the controls to Rose—her body was not responding well enough for her to trust herself with them. Her arms and legs were numb while the rebound drugs forced her G-Shot-thickened blood through the oxygenated fluid in her lungs and to her vital organs.

The Wasp looked whole, but there were no power readings. Beth began to fear that Mercy was right and Bull was dead. She had to make sure, though.

Not that it would matter in the long run, she knew. Back at the gate, Warthog was about to pass through with his precious comms pod. Uncle and Ranger, who were in the same condition as she was, would be next, then Mercy would bring up the rear. Their orders were clear—the gate had to be destroyed, and there was no longer any way that Beth could get there in time. The six remaining alien bogies had not made a move toward the gate, but all of the aliens had managed to remain invisible to Purple Flight before the attack. For all Beth knew, another fighter force was moving to the gate, unseen.

Beth had a bottom aspect of Bull's Wasp. There was the slightest bit of both gamma radiation and mercury leakage from his hadron cannon, but the weapons pods looked undamaged. That pointed to some sort of particle beam weapon instead of a kinetic or laser. Beth ordered Rose to take *Tala* to the other side. As the ship slowly—relative to the other fighter—as they were both still moving at a fast clip to leave the system—swung around Bull's Wasp, Beth contemplated turning her comms back on. She'd cut the connection after too many calls from Mercy and Warthog, trying to convince her to return to the gate. She didn't really have anything to tell them yet, though. It made more sense to wait until she could confirm Bull's death.

The canopy of the Wasp came into view, but Beth couldn't see anything from this angle. She had to get a better view. A Wasp's "canopy" was not a clear bubble as with old-time atmospheric and early spacecraft. It was made of the same material as the skin of the Wasp, fashioned to be able to recess to allow the pilot to enter and exit the cockpit. It had polarizing cells that allowed for full opaqueness for normal operations but would become transparent when the fighter was powered down.

As *Tala* moved to an upper aspect, she could see Bull's helmet and the shoulders of his bright red Stinger flight suit. The rest was lost in the shadows. Bull was not moving, and any hope Beth had evaporated. She had expected it, but she still felt a sense of loss despite the numbness the meds created in her.

"Bring her in to twenty meters, canopy-to-canopy," she told Rose.

She wanted to take a holo shot of him in what would be his tomb, recording his course and speed. She'd pass those back to Mercy. Someday, maybe far into the future, someone might want to track the derelict down and bring Bull home.

Rose brought *Tala* up. The shadows were too severe to see much more, but Bull's helmet looked fine. There was no blood splashed against the inner surface of the canopy. He looked peaceful, and Beth hoped his passing had been painless.

"Fucking hell, Beth! Why did you switch off your comms?" Mercy shouted the second Beth came back up.

Beth ignored the questions, passing the single word "Sending" instead.

"Oh, hell, Beth. We knew it, right? I told you. And now . . ."

"Sending my course as well. I don't intend to deviate," she told her friend.

She knew she was on a one-way trip when she decided to go after Bull, but it was sinking in now. She idly wondered how long it would take for her to die, whether it would be the effects of the G-Shot left untreated or running out of life-support. Hopefully, the rebound meds would keep her from feeling too much regret.

"Beth, you can't just drift on out into the black."

"My choice," she said, keeping it short.

"Uh, no, it's not. You can't . . . we can't let the fighters fall into enemy hands. You need to . . . well . . . you need to destroy Bull's fighter, then you need to get back here now. And if . . . you know . . . if you can't get through the gate in time, you need to self-destruct."

Silence took over the net for a long, long pause.

"I've been told to tell you that we can fire a torp if you can't initiate the self-destruct," Mercy said, her voice catching.

You mean if I don't have the guts.

She understood the reasoning, however. They couldn't let the aliens have access to a Wasp, damaged or not.

"No problem, Mercy. I'm on it."

"But promise me this, Beth," Mercy said in a rush. "Try and get back here, first. We'll hold the gate open as long as we can."

"Is that the official word, Mercy?" Beth asked, her voice calm.

"That's *my* word, sister. And I'll keep it!"

Beth didn't think she would hesitate to initiate the self-destruct, but that could be the drugs talking. Maybe she would. It would kill Mercy to have to fire the torpedo before she went through the gate, and that was something Beth didn't want to lay on her friend.

Her *best* friend.

First things first, though. She had to destroy Bull's Wasp. All she had left was the rail gun, but that would do the job. She had to get much farther away than 20 meters, though, or she could get knocked out by debris—knocked out, but not destroyed.

"Take her out to five klicks, then come about to fire," she said, struggling with the sub-vocalizations.

As *Tala* started to pull forward, she gave one last look above her to Bull's Wasp . . .

. . . and he suddenly looked up as if seeing her for the first time.

"Stop!" she yelled, then went into a fit of coughing.

Bull was waving desperately.

"Can you hear me, Bull?" she asked over the flight net.

"Beth, what's going on?" Mercy asked, and Beth switched to the S2S.

"Bull, can you hear me?" she asked, laboriously bringing a heavy arm up so she could cup her ear.

Bull shook his head, bringing up his hands to his ears as well.

Of course, he can't. He's got no power.

Beth was surprised that Bull was even alive, but she shouldn't be. One of the many reasons that humans were still used in ships was that one of a particle beam's effects, Bremsstrahlung radiation, could fry electronics at relatively low power and yet not kill a person. Beth didn't know the specifics of the alien weapon, nor did she know how far Bull had been when he'd been hit, but it had been far enough for him to survive it. She should have considered the possibility that he was alive inside a dead Wasp.

But what to do now? Fighters didn't have tractor beams. Tugs did, of course, but even if she were in a tug, it would take weeks, if not months, to get his Wasp to the gate.

There was only one choice. Bull had to come to her.

She motioned for him to come over. He didn't hesitate but nodded and gave her a thumbs-up.

Wasp pilots all had to conduct an evac during training, but to a rescue ship, not another Wasp. A fighter wasn't called a single-seat for nothing. There wasn't room for two people. Beth was small, however, and Bull wasn't huge, either. It might not work, but it was their only choice.

Beth had Rose bring *Tala* in closer. Fighter jocks did not have powered suits. They relied on their legs, jumping from their craft to the receiving craft. During training, they had safety spacewalkers all around them to collect errant cadets. Here, it would be just the two of them.

She had *Tala* stop five meters away from him, but held up her hand, palm out, while she ran her checklist, something she hadn't bothered with after the dogfight. It hadn't seemed to matter much one way or the other. Now it did.

Tala had suffered more damage than she'd thought possible. She was mildly surprised the Wasp was still functional. One of the many problems was the integrity of the cockpit. There has been a slow loss of the inert gasses that filled it during combat operations. Normally, that wouldn't matter. O2 was fed into her helmet and was still doing so. But if Bull was going to join her, well, there was only one helmet connection. He'd have to be on cockpit air.

She decided just to go ahead. He was going to die anyway, so why not?

She opened her canopy, the inert gasses escaping in a quick blast of mist. Still strapped in, she then leaned up, arms out to catch him. With a wave of her hand, she beckoned him over. He nodded and pulled the emergency canopy release. His suit itself would have enough air for about three minutes—more than enough time for the crossing, but not enough for her to go chasing him down if he missed. He slid his canopy back, pulled himself into the perfect classroom crouch position, and looked up at her for a moment before launching himself.

He was right on target, crashing through Beth's feeble attempt to catch him and smashing into her chest, knocking the breath out of her. He almost bounced out, but with a death grip on the edge of the open cockpit, he stayed in place.

Between the crunch of bodies and her G-shot, Beth wasn't able to do much, and as he struggled to get his feet inside, he was kicking the heck out of her legs. Finally, he was jammed in, and he hit the canopy closure valve. It started closing as he hugged her tightly, his helmet up against hers. She could see his eyes were huge—whether from panic or adrenaline, she couldn't tell.

The canopy hit his helmet and stopped. His eyes got wider as he struggled to bury his head into her shoulder while scrunching down into the cockpit, but there just wasn't room. It wasn't going to work.

Her hands were trapped, so she banged her helmet on his three times. He turned back to her, and she mouthed, "Take it off."

His eyes got wider, and this time she knew it was panic. Without the helmet, he wouldn't be able to breathe, and if the canopy still wouldn't close, he'd be dead. But if they didn't figure out something, he'd be dead anyway.

"Take your helmet off!" she mouthed again.

With a resigned expression, he nodded, pulling his hands up to his neck release. She watched him hyperventilate, then exhale all the air from his lungs. Looking her right in the eye, he released the helmet and flung it free, out of the cockpit. Panic set in as he hit the canopy closure, and he pushed into her, trying to get his head low. She watched the canopy inch closed, barely clearing his head, and brushing his mohawk as it sealed.

Neither one of them could reach the air release, but she didn't need it. With a quick sub-vocalization, blessed air started to rush in. With something on him pressing under her sternum, she was glad she didn't have to say it aloud.

"Thanks, Ant. I don't know how to thank you. I thought—"

"OK, Bull," she managed to croak out though her helmet mic. "I had to G-Shot."

Each word drained her.

"Rose, accept orders from Warrant Officer Nicolescu, register now."

"I am Chief Warrant Officer Two Taurus Nicolescu," he said immediately.

"Registered."

"G-Shot?" Bull asked.

"Yes. I'm about done. You've got to get us back."

They were slammed together like sardines, but his panic subsided as the professional pilot took over.

"Tuna, I'm alive, thanks to Ant. Need a clear shot to the gate."

"Thank God, Bull. Tuna's gone, Swordfish, too," LTJG Bendick passed. "I don't know if we're going to be able to keep the gate open, but get back here as fast as you can, buddy. Godspeed."

The meds coursing through her body, the strain she'd been put through, and now being crushed by Bull were too much for her. She managed a soft, "Mercy, we're on our way," before, for the second time in the last couple of hours, everything faded to black.

Chapter 14

Beth opened her eyes to Josh sitting in the chair, eyes glued to a reader.

"Don't you have work to do?" she asked.

Her plane captain looked up, a smile taking over his face.

"Not with you off flight status," he said. "Nothing much for me to do until you're out of that bed."

"What about *Tala*? She all ready?"

"She is now, despite all your attempts to wreck her."

"Ha! I took good care of her."

"I'd hate to see what she'd look like if you took bad care of her. Thirty-one modules! Thirty-one I had to replace!"

"I know, I know, you've told me that for the last two days."

"Uh, one thing," he said, suddenly serious.

She looked up, worried by his tone.

"NSP2 Hamlin, she's not going to get charged. She's keeping her flight status, too."

Beth felt a wave of relief sweep over her. It had been touch-and-go. Mercy had demanded that the gate be kept open, threatening anyone with bloody hell if they tried to destroy it before she and Bull made it back. Beth only found out about it after waking up in sickbay, where along with Uncle and Ranger, she was starting her G-Shot convalescence. An outwardly defiant, yet obviously scared Mercy, had told her that there was no case against her. She'd stayed on the other side of the gate, assuring the command that if the aliens appeared heading her way, she would destroy the gate herself, with her on the other side. To her, it was a classic case of no harm, no foul.

Beth had reached out to grab her hand when she heard that, deeply touched, but afraid that the Navy brass wouldn't see it that way. Yet now it seemed as if they had. Beth was pretty sure that the CO had a lot to do with that, pulling in favors from the same GTs who got him his position in the first place.

"I'm glad," she said, a huge understatement.

"Me, too," he said, then added, "Well, if you're awake, do you need anything? Another Coke?"

It seemed that just about everyone in the squadron had stopped by, almost all with a Coke. She'd coked out.

"No, thanks. But there is something. I've been thinking—"

"That's dangerous."

She rolled her eyes and then said, "I've been thinking. I've never really thanked you for your work on *Tala*. She took a lot of abuse, you know, yet somehow she kept on flying. Without you . . . I don't think I'd have made it back."

He lowered his head, stuttered, and managed to mumble out something she didn't quite catch.

"I'm serious, Josh, and I know this isn't much, but maybe you can add your name as plane captain to the nose?"

He looked up, eyes wide open. There was no regulation one way or the other about what went on a fighter's nose. Some pilots had their plane captain's name there as well, but not many. Usually, that was reserved for far more senior captains.

"I'm . . . I'm . . ."

"Just do it, OK? It'll make me happy. And maybe make you pay more attention to what you're doing. Thirty-one modules couldn't stand up to a little fight?"

For once, he didn't have a smart-ass comeback, and she knew he was touched. It was deserved, though. She'd been serious about whether she'd have made it back with someone else keeping *Tala* combat-ready.

He was embarrassed, though, so she took pity on him and said, "maybe I will take that Coke, if you don't mind."

"Your wish is my command," he said, regaining a bit of his old self.

He got up to leave just at the hatch opened and Bull walked in. Josh bristled. He'd been well aware of the warrant officer's antagonism to her, and he blamed the man for almost getting her killed. Like a teacup chihuahua facing down a mastiff, he looked like he was going to block the man from entering.

"It's OK, Josh. Why don't you get that Coke."

With a wary look, Josh edged around Bull, giving him the evil eye before leaving.

"That young man is pretty protective of you," Bull said.

This was the first time she'd seen him since they'd been recovered. She was pretty clear as to what happened to get him into *Tala*, then her memory was in bits and pieces, mostly of him crushing her under him. It had been a relief to finally get pulled out inside the hangar of the cruiser that picked them up.

She'd expected to see him, but thought that he'd have come by before this.

"I trust you're OK, Chief Warrant Officer," she said, her voice cold.

He didn't seem to notice her tone, and he said, "I'm fine, now that I'm out of that stupid ward. The docs say I'll make a full recovery, though." He flexed his hand a few times, then added, "I'm off flight status for a month or so, but that's better than the alternative, right?"

Beth was confused. He hadn't G-shot. Why was he off flight status?

"Why were you with the docs?"

"Because of the nerve damage. Whatever took out *Hammer* almost took me out, too. A little more power in it, and I wouldn't be around anymore." He paused a moment, then said, "And without you, too. I know everyone thought I was a goner. Hell, I knew I was. I expected I'd be out in the deep black by now, waiting until I suffocated or died of thirst."

Beth didn't know what to say, so she stayed silent.

"Look, Ant. Uh . . . Beth. I know I treated you like shit. I thought you were just some PC hire, you know. I thought you got lucky as a civvie pilot, then you got appointed as a petty officer, never earning your way," he got out in a rush.

"Well, I was wrong," he said, his voice choking up. He coughed a few times, clearing his throat, then said, "You're a helluva pilot, Beth, and I'd be proud to have you as a wingman anytime, if you'll ever have me."

Beth had expected him to grudgingly thank her at some time, but this was more than that. He seemed utterly sincere.

"You would have done the same."

"I don't think so. Not before, at least. But now, I would," he said softly, staring at his fingers as if there was something interesting about them.

"Anyway, I just wanted to tell you that before I checked in with Ranger and Uncle. I don't envy you guys," he said with forced humor.

"Thank you. I appreciate it. And I'm not looking forward to this, either. In fact, I'm pretty tired now. If you can, would you tell Frye that I don't want the Coke after all? I want to get some rest."

"He probably won't believe me."

"No, he probably won't."

"Well . . . take it easy, Ant. I'll check in tomorrow, if that's OK."

"Sure. Anytime. I'm not going anywhere," she said before watching him leave.

She wasn't sure why, but a small tear rolled down her cheek.

****

I don't see why I have to come," she told Josh as he wheeled her down the corridor into the hangar.

"Regulations. It's your Wasp, and you have to approve it for the upcheck."

"Not like I'm going to fly anytime soon," she muttered.

It embarrassed her to be wheeled around like an invalid, but the docs wouldn't let her stand until next week, much less start walking again. She wasn't sure she could walk yet even if she wanted to. Navy regulations could be a pain in the butt, though, so it was easier just to let Josh take her there. Hopefully, the place would be empty, she could approve *Tala*, then get back to the ward.

"Where are the lights?" she asked as he pushed her wheelchair into the darkened hangar. "What's going on?"

Josh didn't say a word as he pushed her through the other parked craft before stopping.

"Well, are you going to tell me what game you're playing?" she asked, starting to get a little upset.

She didn't have time for his games now.

Suddenly, a lone light broke through the darkness to illuminate a Wasp. Her Wasp.

"Take a look at the nose," Mercy said, stepping out of the darkness to stand beside her.

"Mercy, what the heck . . ." she started, before trailing off.

At the top, in large script at a 45-degree angle, was "Tala" and a star.

Below that, was "Petty Officer Floribeth S.O. Dalisay, with "Fire Ant" directly beneath.

The bottom line was "Spaceman Josh Frye."

To the left of the names were two images: two odd-looking spacecraft of some kind. It took a moment to realize they symbolized her two enemy kills.

Wow, she thought before she went back to her name.

"Fire Ant?" she asked.

"It was Bull's idea, and everyone agreed. You know, small, but with a wicked fucking bite. If you like it, I mean."

Beth started to protest. She hated "Ant," knowing it was a reference to her size. But "Fire Ant?" It had a . . . something, a cachet. She *was* small, so what? Nothing to be ashamed of. And she did have a bite.

"No, I like it."

Mercy turned around and yelled out, "She likes it!"

Immediately the lights turned on, and the entire squadron came out from hiding with a cheer. They rushed her, waiting to shake her hand.

"Holy crap!"

"Beth, you cursing? I'm fucking surprised at you!" Mercy said with a laugh.

Beth sat in her chair, just gaping at everyone. Several people carried glasses of Coke from what looked to be a Coke fountain on one of the tech tables. She took one, but immediately spilled it as people reached out to shake her hand.

Towering above the rest, but in the back, was the Dark Knight himself. She caught his eye, and Commander Tuominen nodded.

Beth had felt like an outsider since arriving. She wasn't one of them, and except with Mercy and Josh, she didn't think she'd ever fit in. That had changed. She'd found a home. More than that, she was a Wasp pilot, a *fucking* great Wasp pilot, and with the enemy out there, her services were going to be needed.

Her story had just begun.

Thank you for reading *Fire Ant*. I hope you enjoyed the book, and I welcome a review on Amazon, Goodreads, or any other outlet.

If you would like updates on new books releases, news, or special offers, please consider signing up for my mailing list. Your email will not be sold, rented, or in any other way disseminated. If you are interested, please sign up at the link below:

http://eepurl.com/bnFSHH

OTHER BOOKS BY JONATHAN BRAZEE

The Navy of Humankind: Wasp Squadron
Fire Ant

The United Federation Marine Corps
Recruit
Sergeant
Lieutenant
Captain
Major
Lieutenant Colonel
Colonel
Commandant

Rebel
(Set in the UFMC universe.)

Behind Enemy Lines
(A UFMC Prequel)

The Accidental War (A Ryck Lysander Short Story Published
in *BOB's Bar: Tales from the Multiverse*)

The United Federation Marine Corps' Lysander Twins
Legacy Marines
Esther's Story: Recon Marine
Noah's Story: Marine Tanker
Esther's Story: Special Duty
Blood United

Coda

Women of the United Federation Marine Corps
Gladiator
Sniper
Corpsman

High Value Target (A Gracie Medicine Crow Short Story)
BOLO Mission (A Gracie Medicine Crow Short Story)
Weaponized Math (A Gracie Medicine Crow Novelette, Published in *The Expanding Universe 3*)

The United Federation Marine Corps' Grub Wars
Alliance
The Price of Honor
Division of Power

GHOST MARINES
Integration

The Return of the Marines Trilogy
The Few
The Proud
The Marines

The Al Anbar Chronicles: First Marine Expeditionary Force--Iraq
Prisoner of Fallujah
Combat Corpsman
Sniper

Werewolf of Marines
Werewolf of Marines: Semper Lycanus
Werewolf of Marines: Patria Lycanus
Werewolf of Marines: Pax Lycanus

To the Shores of Tripoli

Wererat

Darwin's Quest: The Search for the Ultimate Survivor

Venus: A Paleolithic Short Story

Secession

Duty
Semper Fidelis

Non-Fiction

Exercise for a Longer Life

Author Website
http://www.jonathanbrazee.com

86624479R00084

Made in the USA
San Bernardino, CA
29 August 2018